Missing Person

Missing Person

by
Patrick Modiano

---

translated by
Daniel Weissbort

JONATHAN CAPE
THIRTY BEDFORD SQUARE LONDON

First published in Great Britain 1980
This translation © Jonathan Cape Ltd, 1980
Jonathan Cape Ltd, 30 Bedford Square, London WC1

First published in French 1978,
under the title *Rue des Boutiques Obscures*
© Éditions Gallimard, 1978

British Library Cataloguing in Publication Data

Modiano, Patrick
Missing person.
I. Title
843'.9'1F   PQ2673.03R8

ISBN 0-224-01789-6

Photoset in Great Britain by
Rowland Phototypesetting Ltd, Bury St Edmunds, Suffolk
and printed by St Edmundsbury Press
Bury St Edmunds, Suffolk

For Rudy
For my father

I

I am nothing. Nothing but a pale shape, silhouetted that evening against the café terrace, waiting for the rain to stop; the shower had started when Hutte left me.

Some hours before, we had met again for the last time on the premises of the Agency. Hutte, as usual, sat at his massive desk, but with his coat on, so that there was really an air of departure about it. I sat opposite him, in the leather armchair we kept for clients. The opaline lamp shed a bright light which dazzled me.

'Well, there we are, Guy . . . That's it . . . ', said Hutte, with a sigh.

A stray file lay on the desk. Maybe it was the one belonging to the dark little man with the frightened expression and the puffy face, who had hired us to follow his wife. In the afternoon, she met another dark little man with a puffy face, at a residential hotel, in the Rue Vital, close to the Avenue Paul-Doumer.

Thoughtfully, Hutte stroked his beard, a grizzly, close cut beard, but one which spread out over his cheeks. His large, limpid eyes stared dreamily ahead. To the left of the desk, the wicker chair where I sat during working hours. Behind Hutte, dark wooden shelves covered half the wall: there were rows of street-and-trade directories and year-books of all kinds, going back over the last fifty years. Hutte had often told me that these were the essential tools of the trade and that

he would never part with them. And that these directories and year-books constituted the most valuable and
moving library you could imagine, as their pages listed
people, things, vanished worlds, to which they alone
bore witness.

'What will you do with all these directories?' I asked
Hutte, taking in the shelves with a sweeping gesture.

'I'm leaving them here, Guy. I'm keeping the lease on
the apartment.'

He cast a swift glance around. The double door
leading into the small adjoining room was open and one
could see the worn, velvet-covered sofa, the fire-place,
and the mirror in which the rows of year-books and
directories and Hutte's face were reflected. Our clients
often waited in this room. A Persian carpet protected the
parquet floor. An icon hung on the wall, near the
window.

'What are you thinking about, Guy?'

'Nothing. So, you're keeping the lease?'

'Yes. I'll be coming back to Paris from time to time
and the Agency will be my *pied-à-terre*.'

He held out his cigarette case.

'I think it's less sad if I keep the place as it is.'

We had been working together for over eight years.
He himself had started this private detective agency in
1947 and had worked with quite a number of other
people before me. Our business was supplying clients
with what Hutte called 'society information'. It was all,
as he was fond of repeating, a matter of dealings
between 'society folk'.

'Do you think you'll be able to live in Nice?'

'Of course.'

'You won't get bored?'

He blew out some smoke.

'One has to retire eventually, Guy.'

He rose heavily. Hutte must be over six feet tall and
weigh more than 15 stone.

'My train's at 20.55. We've time for a drink.'

He walked ahead of me into the corridor which leads to the entrance hall, an odd, oval-shaped room with pale-beige-coloured walls. A black portfolio, so full that it would not close, was standing on the floor. Hutte picked it up. He carried it, one hand underneath.

'You've no luggage?'

'I sent everything on ahead.'

Hutte opened the front door and I switched off the hall light. On the landing, Hutte paused a moment before shutting the door and the metallic sound cut me to the quick. It marked the end of a long period in my life.

'It is a sad business, isn't it Guy?' said Hutte, and he took a large handkerchief from his coat pocket and mopped his brow.

The black marble rectangular plaque, with its gilt and pailletted lettering, was still there:

C. M. HUTTE
Private Enquiries

'I'm leaving it,' said Hutte.

Then he turned the key in the lock.

We walked along the Avenue Niel as far as the Place Pereire. It was dark and, though winter was not far off, the air was still mild. In the Place Pereire, we sat down on the terrace of the Hortensias. Hutte liked this café, because of the fluted chairs – 'just like the old days'.

'And what about you, Guy, what are you going to do?' he asked, after he had gulped down some brandy and soda.

'Me? I'm following something up.'

'Following something up?'

'Yes. My past.'

I had said this rather portentously and it made him smile.

9

'I always thought that one day you'd try to find your past again.'

Now he was serious and I was touched by it.

'But look here, Guy, I wonder if it's really worth it.'

He fell silent. What was he thinking of? His own past?

'I'll give you a key to the Agency. You can go there from time to time. I'd like that.'

He held out a key, which I slid into my trouser pocket.

'And call me in Nice. Let me know what's happening, how you're getting on . . . with your past . . . '

He rose and clasped my hand.

'Shall I go with you to the station?'

'No, no . . . It's so sad . . . '

With a single stride he was out of the café, not turning round, and I felt an emptiness all of a sudden. This man had meant a lot to me. Without him, without his help, I wonder what would have become of me, ten years back, when I was struck by amnesia and was groping about in a fog. He had been moved by my case and, through his many contacts, had even managed to procure me a civil status.

'Here,' he had said, handing me a large envelope which contained an identity card and a passport. 'Your name is "Guy Roland" now.'

And this private detective whose professional services I had sought in uncovering witnesses or traces of my past, had added:

'My dear "Guy Roland", from here on don't look back, think only of the present and the future. How about working with me? . . . '

If he felt drawn to me, it was because he too – I learnt later – had lost track of himself and a whole section of his life had been engulfed without leaving the slightest trace, the slightest connection that could still link him with the past. Because what was there in common between this tired old man whom I watched moving off into the night in his threadbare coat and carrying a big black portfolio, and the handsome tennis player of days gone by, the flaxen-haired Baltic Baron, Constantin von Hutte?

2

'Hello. Is that Mr Paul Sonachidze?'

'Speaking.'

'This is Guy Roland . . . You know, the . . . '

'Yes, of course! I know. Can we meet?'

'If you will . . . '

'What about . . . this evening, around nine, Rue Anatole-de-la-Forge? . . . Is that all right?'

'Yes.'

'I'll expect you. See you later!'

He hung up abruptly and the sweat was running down my temples. I had drunk a glass of cognac to steady myself. Why did a harmless act like dialling a phone number cause me so much anguish?

There were no customers in the bar, in the Rue Anatole-de-la-Forge, and he was standing behind the counter, dressed in his outdoor clothes.

'You're in luck,' he said. 'I've every Wednesday evening off.'

He approached me and put his hand on my shoulder.

'I've thought a lot about you.'

'Thanks.'

'It's really been on my mind, you know . . . '

I wanted to tell him not to worry, but the words failed me.

'I've come to the conclusion that you must have been a friend of someone I used to see a lot of at one time . . . But who?'

He shook his head.

'You can't give me a clue?' he asked.

'No.'

'Why not?'

'I don't remember.'

He thought I was joking and, as if this were a game or a riddle, he said:

'All right. I'll manage on my own. But can I have a free hand?'

'As you wish.'

'This evening, then, I'm taking you out to dinner at a friend's.'

Before leaving, he pulled down the lever of an electric meter firmly and closed the heavy wooden door, turning the key several times in the lock.

His car was parked on the other side of the street. It was black and new. He opened the door for me courteously.

'This friend of mine manages a very pleasant restaurant on the edge of Ville-d'Avray and Saint-Cloud.'

'So far?'

'Yes.'

From the Rue Anatole-de-la-Forge, we emerged into the Avenue de la Grande-Armée and I was tempted to jump out. Ville-d'Avray seemed impossibly far to me. But I held myself back.

Until we reached the Porte de Saint-Cloud, I had to struggle with the panic fear that gripped me. I hardly knew this Sonachidze. Wasn't he drawing me into a trap? But gradually, as I listened to his talk, I grew calmer. He told me about the different stages of his professional life. First he had worked in the Russian night clubs, then at Langer's, a restaurant on the Champs-Elysées, then at the Hôtel Castille, Rue Cambon, and he had worked in other establishments too, before taking over the bar in the Rue Anatole-de-la-Forge. Periodically he met Jean Heurteur, the friend we were going to see, so that, over twenty years, the two of them had formed a tandem. Heurteur too remembered things. Together, they would certainly solve the 'riddle' I was posing.

Sonachidze drove with extreme caution and it took us almost three-quarters of an hour to arrive at our destination.

A kind of bungalow, a weeping willow masking its left side. On the right, I could see a jumble of bushes. The interior of the restaurant was huge. A man came striding towards us from the back, where a bright light shone. He held out his hand to me.

'Glad to meet you, sir. I am Jean Heurteur.'

Then addressing Sonachidze:

'Hello, Paul.'

He led us towards the back of the room. There was a table, laid for three, with flowers in the middle.

He pointed to one of the french windows:

'I've got customers in the other bungalow. A wedding-party.'

'You've never been here before?' Sonachidze asked me.

'No.'

'Show him the view, then, Jean.'

Heurteur preceded me on to a veranda which over-looked a pond. To the left, a small hump-back bridge, in the Chinese style, led to another bungalow, on the other side of the pond. The french windows were brilliantly lit up and I could see couples moving behind them. They were dancing. Snatches of music reached us.

'It's not a large crowd,' he said, 'and I've the feeling this wedding-party is going to end in an orgy.'

He shrugged his shoulders.

'You should come here in summer. We dine out on the veranda. It's pleasant.'

We went back inside the restaurant and Heurteur closed the french windows.

'I've prepared a simple little meal.'

He motioned to us to be seated. They sat side by side, facing me.

'What would you like to drink?' Heurteur asked me.

'You choose.'

'Château-Petrus?'

'An excellent choice, Jean,' said Sonachidze.

A young man in a white jacket waited on us. The light from the bracket-lamp fell directly on me and dazzled me. The others were in shadow, but no doubt they had seated me there so as to be able to study me better.

'Well, Jean?'

Heurteur had started on his galantine and from time to time cast a sharp glance at me. He was dark-skinned, like Sonachidze, and like the latter dyed his hair. Blotchy, flabby cheeks and the thin lips of a gourmet.

'Yes, yes . . . ,' he murmured.

The light made me blink. He poured us some wine.

'Yes . . . I do believe I have seen this gentleman before . . . '

'It's a real puzzle,' said Sonachidze. 'He won't give us any clues . . . '

A thought suddenly seemed to strike him.

'But perhaps you'd rather we didn't talk about it any more? Would you prefer to remain incognito?'

'Not at all,' I said with a smile.

The young man brought us a serving of sweetbreads.

'What business are you in?' asked Heurteur.

'For eight years I've been working in a private detective agency, the C. M. Hutte Agency.'

They stared at me in amazement.

'But I'm sure that's got nothing to do with my previous life. So, don't worry about it.'

'Strange,' announced Heurteur, gazing at me, 'it's hard to tell your age.'

'Because of the moustache, no doubt.'

'Without your moustache,' said Sonachidze, 'perhaps we'd know you right away.'

And he held out his arm, placed the open palm of his

14

hand just under my nose to hide the moustache and screwed up his eyes like a portrait painter in front of his model.

'The more I see of this gentleman, the more it seems to me he was in that crowd . . . ' said Heurteur.

'But when?' asked Sonachidze.

'Oh . . . a long time ago . . . It's ages since we've worked in the night clubs, Paul . . . '

'Do you think it goes back to the time we worked at the Tanagra?'

Heurteur stared at me more and more intently.

'Excuse me,' he said, 'but would you stand up for a moment?'

I did as he asked. He looked me up and down a couple of times.

'Yes, you do remind me of a certain customer. Your height . . . Just a moment . . . '

He had raised his hand and was sitting quite still, as if trying to hold on to some fleeting memory.

'Just one moment . . . Just one moment . . . I have it, Paul . . . '

He smiled triumphantly.

'You can sit down . . . '

He was jubilant. He was sure of the effect of what he was about to say. Ceremoniously he poured out some wine for Sonachidze and me.

'You were always with a man, as tall as yourself . . . perhaps even taller . . . Do you remember, Paul?'

'What period are we talking about, though?' asked Sonachidze.

'The Tanagra, of course . . . '

'A man as tall as himself?' Sonachidze repeated. 'At the Tanagra? . . . '

'Don't you see?'

Heurteur shrugged his shoulders.

Now it was Sonachidze's turn to smile triumphantly. He nodded.

'I do see . . . '

'Well?'

'Styoppa.'

'Yes, of course, Styoppa . . . '

Sonachidze had turned to me.

'Did you know Styoppa?'

'Perhaps,' I said carefully.

'Of course you did . . . ,' said Heurteur. 'You were often with Styoppa . . . I'm sure of it . . . '

'Styoppa . . . '

Judging from the way Sonachidze pronounced it, evidently a Russian name.

'He was the one who always asked the band to play "Alaverdi" . . . ' said Heurteur. 'A Caucasian song . . . '

'Do you remember?' said Sonachidze, gripping my wrist very hard. ' "Alaverdi" . . . '

He whistled the tune, his eyes shining. Suddenly, I too was moved. The tune seemed familiar to me.

Just then, the waiter who had served us approached Heurteur and indicated something at the far end of the room.

A woman was seated alone at one of the tables, in semi-darkness. She was wearing a pale blue dress and her chin was cupped in the palms of her hands. What was she dreaming of?

'The bride.'

'What is she doing there?' asked Heurteur.

'I don't know,' said the waiter.

'Did you ask her if she wanted anything?'

'No. No. She doesn't want anything.'

'And the others?'

'They ordered another dozen bottles of Krugg.'

Heurteur shrugged.

'It's none of my business.'

And Sonachidze, who had taken no notice of 'the bride', or of what they were saying, kept repeating:

'Yes . . . Styoppa . . . Do you remember Styoppa?'

He was so excited that I ended up answering, with a smile that was intended to be enigmatic:

'Yes, yes. A little . . . '

He turned to Heurteur and said in a grave tone:

'He remembers Styoppa.'

'Just as I thought.'

The white-coated waiter stood quite still in front of Heurteur, looking embarrassed.

'I think they're going to use the rooms, sir . . . What should I do?'

'I knew this wedding-party would end badly,' said Heurteur. 'Well, old chap, they can do what they like. It's none of our business.'

The bride sat motionless at the table. She had crossed her arms.

'I wonder why she's sitting there on her own,' said Heurteur. 'Anyway, it's got absolutely nothing to do with us . . . '

And he flicked his hand, as though brushing a fly away.

'Let's get back to business', he said. 'You admit then you knew Styoppa?'

'Yes,' I sighed.

'In other words, you were in the same crowd . . . They were quite a crowd too, weren't they, Paul . . . ?'

'Oh . . . ! They've all gone now,' said Sonachidze gloomily. 'Except for you, sir . . . I'm delighted to have been able to . . . to place you . . . You were in Styoppa's crowd . . . You were lucky! . . . Those were much better times than now, and people were better class too . . . '

'And what's more, we were younger,' said Heurteur, laughing.

'When are you talking about?' I asked them, my heart pounding.

'We're not good at dates,' said Sonachidze. 'But, in any case, it goes back to the beginning of time, all that . . . '

Suddenly he seemed exhausted.

'There certainly are some strange coincidences,' said Heurteur.

And he got up, went over to a little bar in a corner of the room, and brought back a newspaper, turning over the pages. Finally, he handed me the paper, pointing to the following notice:

The death is announced of Marie de Rosen, on October 25th, in her ninety-second year.

On behalf of her daughter, her son, her grandsons, nephews and grand-nephews.

And on behalf of her friends, George Sacher and Styoppa de Dzhagorev.

A service, followed by the interment in the Sainte-Geneviève-des-Bois Cemetery, will take place, on November 4th, at 16.00 h. in the cemetery chapel.

Ninth Day Divine Service will be held on November 5th, in the Russian Orthodox Church, 19 Rue Claude-Lorrain, 75016, Paris.

'Please take this announcement as the only notification.'

'So, Styoppa is alive?' said Sonachidze. 'Do you still see him?'

'No,' I said.

'You're right. One must live in the present. Jean, how about a brandy?'

'Good idea.'

From then on, they seemed completely to lose interest in Styoppa and my past. But it made no difference, since at last I was on the track.

'Can I keep the paper?' I asked casually.

'Certainly,' said Heurteur.

We clinked glasses. All that was left of what I had once been, then, was a dim shape in the minds of two bartenders, and even that was almost obliterated by the memory of a certain Styoppa de Dzhagorev. And they had heard nothing of this Styoppa since 'the beginning of time', as Sonachidze said.

'So, you're a private detective?' Heurteur asked me.

'Not any more. My employer has just retired.'

'And are you carrying on?'

I shrugged and did not answer.

'Anyway, I should be delighted to see you again. Come back any time.'

He had got to his feet and held out his hand to us.

'Excuse me for showing you out now, but I've still my accounts to do . . . And those others with their . . . orgy.'

He gestured in the direction of the pond.

'Good-bye, Jean.'

'Good-bye, Paul.'

Heurteur looked at me thoughtfully. Speaking very softly:

'Now that you're standing, you remind me of something else . . . '

'What does he remind you of?' asked Sonachidze.

'A customer who used to come every evening, very late, when we worked at the Hôtel Castille . . . '

Sonachidze, in his turn, looked me up and down.

'It's possible,' he said, 'that you're an old customer from the Hôtel Castille after all . . . '

I gave an embarrassed smile.

Sonachidze took my arm and we crossed the restaurant, which was even darker than when we had arrived. The bride in the pale blue dress was no longer at her table. Outside, we heard blasts of music and laughter coming from across the pond.

'Could you please remind me what that song was that this . . . this . . . '

'Styoppa?' asked Sonachidze.

'Yes, which he always asked for . . . '

He started whistling the first few bars. Then he stopped.

'Will you see Styoppa again?'

'Perhaps.'

He gripped my arm very hard.

'Tell him Sonachidze still thinks of him a lot.'

His gaze lingered on me:

'Maybe Jean's right after all. You were a customer at the Hôtel Castille . . . Try to remember . . . The Hôtel Castille, Rue Cambon . . .'

I turned away and opened the car door. Someone was huddled up on the front seat, leaning against the window. I bent down and recognized the bride. She was asleep, her pale blue dress drawn up to the middle of her thighs.

'We'll have to get her out of there,' said Sonachidze.

I shook her gently but she went on sleeping. So, I took her by the waist and managed to pull her out of the car.

'We can't just leave her on the ground,' I said.

I carried her in my arms to the restaurant. Her head lay against my shoulder and her fair hair caressed my neck. She was wearing some highly pungent perfume which reminded me of something. But what?

3

It was a quarter to six. I asked the taxi driver to wait for me in the little Rue Charles-Marie-Widor and proceeded on foot until I reached the Rue Claude-Lorrain, where the Russian Church was.

A detached, one-storey building, with net curtains at the windows. On the right, a very wide path. I took up my position on the pavement facing it.

First I saw two women who stopped in front of the door opening on to the street. One had short brown hair and wore a black woollen shawl; the other was a blonde, very made up, and sported a grey hat which was shaped like a Musketeer's. I heard them speaking French.

A stout, elderly man, completely bald, with heavy bags under his Mongolian slits of eyes, extracted himself from a taxi. They started up the path.

On the left, from the Rue Boileau, a group of five people came towards me. In front, two middle-aged women supported a very old man by the arms, an old man so white-haired, so fragile, he seemed to be made of dried plaster. There followed two men who looked alike, father and son no doubt, both wearing well-cut, grey striped suits, the father dandified, the son with wavy blond hair. Just at this moment, a car braked level with the group and another alert, stiff old man, enveloped in a loden cape, his grey hair cut short, got out. He had a military bearing. Was this Styoppa?

They all entered the church by a side door, at the end of the path. I would have liked to have followed them, but my presence among them would have attracted attention. I was having increasing qualms that I might fail to identify Styoppa.

A car had just pulled to one side, a little further off, on the right. Two men got out, then a woman. One of the men was very tall and wore a navy-blue overcoat. I crossed the street and waited for them.

They come closer and closer. It seems to me that the tall man stares hard at me before starting up the path with the two others. Behind the stained glass windows which look out on to the path, tapers are burning. He stoops as he passes through the door, which is much too low for him, and I know it is Styoppa.

The taxi's engine was running but there was no one at the wheel. One of the doors was ajar, as if the driver would be returning any moment. Where could he be? I glanced about me and decided to walk round the block to look for him.

I found him in a café close by, in the Rue Chardon-Lagache. He was seated at a table, with a glass of beer in front of him.

'Are you going to be much longer?' he asked.

'Oh . . . another twenty minutes.'

Fair-haired, pale-skinned, with heavy jowls and protruding eyes. I don't think I have ever seen a man with fleshier ear lobes.

'Does it matter if I let the meter run?'

'It doesn't matter,' I said.

He smiled politely.

'Aren't you afraid your taxi might get stolen?'

He shrugged his shoulders.

'Oh, you know . . . '

He had ordered a pâté sandwich and was eating with deliberation, gazing at me gloomily.

'What exactly are you waiting for?'

'Someone who'll be coming out of the Russian Church, down the road.'

'Are you Russian?'

'No.'

'It's silly . . . You should have asked him when he was leaving . . . It would have cost you less . . . '

'Never mind.'

He ordered another glass of beer.

'Could you get me a paper?' he said.

He started searching in his pocket for the change, but I stopped him.

'Don't worry . . . '

'Thanks. Get me *Le Hérisson*. Thanks again . . . '

I wandered about for quite a while before finding a newsagent in the Avenue de Versailles. *Le Hérisson* was printed on a creamy green paper.

He read, knitting his brows and turning over the pages after moistening his index finger with his tongue. And I contemplated this fat, blond, blue-eyed man, with white skin, reading his green paper.

I didn't dare interrupt him in his reading. At last, he consulted his tiny wrist watch.

'We must go.'

In the Rue Charles-Marie-Widor, he sat down behind

the wheel of his taxi and I asked him to wait for me. Again, I stationed myself in front of the Russian Church, but on the opposite side of the street.

There was no one there. Had they, perhaps, left already? If so, there was no hope of my tracking down Styoppa de Dzhagorev again, since his name was not in the Paris directory. The tapers still burnt behind the stained glass windows which looked out on to the path. Had I known the ancient lady for whom this service was being held? If I had been one of Styoppa's frequent companions, he would probably have introduced me to his friends, including, no doubt, this Marie de Rosen. She must have been far older than us at the time.

The door they had entered by and which must have led into the chapel where the ceremony was taking place, this door which I was keeping under constant watch, suddenly opened, and the blonde woman in the Musketeer's hat stood framed in it. The brunette in the black shawl followed. Then the father and son, in their grey striped suits, supporting the plaster figure of the old man, who was talking to the fat bald-headed man with the Mongolian features. And the latter was stooping, his ear practically touching his companion's lips: the old gentleman's voice must certainly have been hardly more than a whisper. Others followed. I was watching for Styoppa, my heart pounding.

Finally, he emerged, among the last. His great height and navy-blue overcoat allowed me to keep him in sight, as there was a large number of them, forty at least. They were mostly getting on in years, but I noticed a few young women and even children. They all lingered on the path, talking among themselves.

The scene resembled a country school playground. The old man with the plaster appearance was installed on a bench, and each of them in turn came up to greet him. Who was he? 'George Sacher', mentioned in the newspaper notice? Or an ex-graduate of the College of Pages? Perhaps he and Marie de Rosen had lived out some brief idyll in Petersburg, or on the shores of the Black Sea, before everything fell to pieces? The fat bald-headed man with the Mongolian eyes was surrounded by people as well. The father and son, in their grey striped suits, circulated, like a pair of dancers at some society ball, moving from table to table. They seemed full of themselves, and the father kept breaking into laughter, throwing back his head, which I found incongruous.

Styoppa, for his part, was talking soberly with the woman in the grey Musketeer's hat. He laid his hand on her arm and on her shoulder in a courtly and affectionate manner. He must have been a very handsome man. I put him down as seventy. His face was a little bloated, his hair receding, but the prominent nose and the set of the head I found extremely noble. Or such was my impression from a distance.

Time passed. Almost half an hour had gone by and they were still talking. I was afraid that one of them would finally notice me, standing there on the pavement. And the taxi driver? I strode back to the Rue Charles-Marie-Widor. The engine was still running and he was seated at the wheel, deep in his yellowy green paper.

'Well?' he asked me.

'I don't know,' I said. 'We might have to wait another hour.'

'Hasn't your friend come out of the church yet?'

'Yes, but he's chatting with the others.'

'You can't ask him to come?'

'No.'

His large blue eyes stared at me in consternation.

'Don't worry,' I said.

'It's for you . . . I have to keep the meter running . . . '

I returned to my post, opposite the Russian Church.

Styoppa had advanced a few feet. As a matter of fact, he was no longer standing at the end of the path but on the pavement, in the centre of a group consisting of the blonde woman in the Musketeer's hat, the brunette in the black shawl, the bald-headed man with the slanted Mongolian eyes, and two other men.

This time I crossed the street and stationed myself close to them, my back turned. The soft bursts of Russian filled the air and I wondered if a deeper, more resonant voice among them was Styoppa's. I turned round. He gave the blonde woman in the Musketeer's hat a long embrace. He was almost shaking her, and his features contracted in a painful grin. Then, in the same fashion, he embraced the fat bald-headed man with the slant eyes, and each of the others in turn. The time for farewells, I thought. I ran back to the taxi and jumped in.

'Quick . . . straight ahead . . . in front of the Russian Church . . . '

Styoppa was still talking to them.

'Do you see the tall chap in navy-blue?'

'Yes.'

'We'll have to follow him, if he's in a car.'

The driver turned round, stared at me, and his blue eyes opened wide.

'I hope it's not dangerous, sir.'

'Don't worry,' I said.

Styoppa detached himself from the group, walked a few paces and, without turning, waved his arm. The others, standing still, watched him. The woman in the grey Musketeer's hat stood slightly to the front of the group, arched, like the figurehead of a ship, the large feather of her hat fluttering gently in the breeze.

He took some time opening the door of his car. I think he tried the wrong key. When he was seated at the wheel, I leant forward to the taxi driver.

'Follow the car which the chap in navy-blue has got into.'

And I hoped I wasn't off on a false trail, since there was nothing really to indicate that this man was Styoppa de Dzhagorev.

4

It was not very hard to follow him: he drove slowly. At the Porte Maillot, he ran a red light and the taxi driver did not dare follow suit, but we caught up with him again at the Boulevard Maurice-Barrès. Our two cars drew level with each other at a pedestrian crossing. He glanced across at me absentmindedly, as motorists do when they find themselves side by side in a traffic jam.

He parked his car on the Boulevard Richard-Wallace, in front of the apartment buildings at the end, near the Pont de Puteaux and the Seine. He started down the Rue Julien-Potin and I paid off my taxi.

'Good luck, sir,' said the driver. 'Be careful . . . '

And I felt his eyes following me as I too started down the Rue Julien-Potin. Perhaps he thought I was in some danger.

Night was falling. A narrow road, lined by impersonal apartment buildings, built between the wars, which formed a single long façade, on each side and all the way along the Rue Julien-Potin. Styoppa was ten yards ahead of me. He turned right into the Rue Ernest-Deloison, and entered a grocer's shop.

The moment had come to approach him. But because of my shyness it was extremely hard for me, and I was afraid he would take me for a madman: I would stammer, my speech would become incoherent. Unless he recognized me at once, in which case I would let him do the talking.

He was coming out of the grocer's shop, holding a paper bag.

'Mr Styoppa de Dzhagorev?'

He looked very surprised. Our heads were on the same level, which intimidated me even more.

'Yes. But who are you?'

No, he did not recognize me. He spoke French without an accent. I had to screw up my courage.

'I . . . I've been meaning to contact you for . . . a long time . . . '

'What for?'

'I am writing . . . writing a book about the Emigration . . . I . . . '

'Are you Russian?'

It was the second time I had been asked this question. The taxi driver too had asked me. And, actually, perhaps I had been Russian.

'No.'

'And you're interested in the Emigration?'

'I . . . I . . . I'm writing a book about the Emigration. Some . . . someone suggested I came to see you . . . Paul Sonachidze . . . '

'Sonachidze? . . . '

He pronounced the name in the Russian way. It was very soft, like wind rustling in the trees.

'A Georgian name . . . I don't know it . . . '

He frowned.

'Sonachidze . . . no . . . '

'I don't want to be a nuisance. If I could just ask you a few questions.'

'I'd be happy to answer them . . . '

He smiled a sad smile.

'A tragic tale, the Emigration . . . But how is it you call me Styoppa? . . . '

'I . . . don't . . . I . . . '

'Most of those who called me Styoppa are dead. The others, you can count on the fingers of one hand.'

'It was . . . Sonachidze . . . '

'I don't know him.'

'Can I . . . ask . . . you . . . a few questions?'

'Yes. Would you like to come up to my place? We can talk.'

In the Rue Julien-Potin, after we had passed through

27

a gateway, we crossed an open space surrounded by apartment buildings. We took a wooden lift with a double lattice-work gate and, because of our height and the restricted space in the lift, we had to bow our heads and keep them turned towards the wall, so we didn't knock brows.

He lived on the fifth floor in a two-room flat. He showed me into the bedroom and stretched out on the bed.

'Forgive me,' he said, 'but the ceiling is too low. It's suffocating to stand.'

Indeed, there were only a few inches between the ceiling and the top of my head and I had to stoop. Furthermore, both he and I were a head too tall to clear the frame of the door leading into the other room and I imagined that he had often bumped his forehead there.

'You can stretch out too . . . if you wish . . . ' He pointed to a small couch, upholstered in pale blue velvet, near the window.

'Make yourself at home . . . you'll be much more comfortable lying down . . . Even if you sit, you feel cooped up here . . . Please, do lie down . . . '

I did so.

He had switched on a lamp with a salmon-pink shade, which was standing on his bedside table, and it gave out a soft light and cast shadows on the ceiling.

'So, you're interested in the Emigration?'

'Very.'

'And yet, you're still young . . . '

Young? I had never thought of myself as young. A large mirror in a gold frame hung on the wall, close to me. I looked at my face. Young?

'Oh . . . not so young as all that . . . '

There was a moment's silence. The two of us, stretched out on either side of the room, looked like opium smokers.

'I've just returned from a funeral,' he said. 'It's a pity you didn't meet the old lady who died . . . She could

28

have told you many things . . . She was one of the real
personalities of the Emigration . . . '

'Really?'

'A very brave woman. At the beginning, she opened a
small tea-room, in the Rue du Mont-Thabor, and she
helped everybody . . . It was very hard . . . '

He sat up on the edge of the bed, his back bowed,
arms crossed.

'I was fifteen at the time . . . When I think, there are
not many left . . . '

'There's . . . George Sacher . . . ,' I said at random.

'Not for much longer. Do you know him?'

Was it the old gentleman of plaster? Or the fat
bald-head with the Mongolian features?

'Look,' he said, 'I can't go over all these things again
. . . It makes me too sad . . . But I can show you some
photographs . . . The names and dates are there on the
back . . . You'll manage on your own . . . '

'It's very kind of you to take so much trouble.'

He smiled at me.

'I've got lots of photos . . . I wrote the names and
dates on the back, because one forgets everything . . . '

He stood up and, stooping, went into the next room.

I heard him open a drawer. He returned, a large red
box in his hand, sat down on the floor and leant his back
against the edge of the bed.

'Come and sit down beside me. It will be easier to
look at the photographs.'

I did so. A confectioner's name was printed in gothic
lettering on the lid of the box. He opened it. It was full
of photos.

'In here you have the principal figures of the
Emigration,' he said.

He handed me the photographs one by one, telling
me the names and dates he read on the back: it was a
litany, to which the Rusian names lent a particular
resonance, now explosive like cymbals clashing, now
plaintive or almost mute. Trubetskoy. Orbelyani.

Sheremetev. Galitsyn. Eristov. Obolensky. Bagration. Chavchavadze . . . Now and then, he took a photo back and consulted the name and date again. Some occasion. The Grand Duke Boris's table at a gala ball at the Château-Basque, long after the Revolution. And this garland of faces on a photograph taken at a 'black and white' dinner party, in 1914 . . . A class photograph of the Alexander Lycée in Petersburg.

'My older brother . . . '

He handed me the photos more and more quickly, no longer even looking at them. Evidently, he was anxious to have done with it. Suddenly I halted at one of them, printed on heavier paper than the others, and with no explanation on the back.

'What is it?' he asked me. 'Something puzzling you?'

In the foreground, an old man, stiff and smiling, seated in an armchair. Behind him, a blonde young woman with very limpid eyes. All around, small groups of people, most of whom had their backs to the camera. And towards the left, his right arm cut off by the edge of the picture, his hand on the shoulder of the blonde young woman, an extremely tall man, in a broken check lounge suit, about thirty years old, with dark hair and a thin moustache. I was convinced it was me.

I drew closer to him. Our backs leant against the edge of the bed, our legs were stretched out on the floor, our shoulders touched.

'Tell me, who are those people?' I asked him.

He took the photograph and looked at it wearily.

'That one was Giorgiadze . . . '

He pointed to the old man, seated in the armchair.

'He was at the Georgian Consulate in Paris, up to the time . . . '

He did not finish his sentence, as though its conclusion must be obvious to me.

'That one was his grand-daughter . . . Her name was Gay . . . Gay Orlov. She emigrated to America with her parents . . . '

'Did you know her?'

'Not very well. No. She stayed on in America a long time.'

'And what about him?' I asked in a toneless voice, pointing to myself in the photo.

'Him?'

He knitted his brows.

'I don't know who he is.'

'Really?'

'No.'

I sighed deeply.

'Don't you think he looks like me?'

He looked at me.

'Looks like you? No. Why?'

'Nothing.'

He handed me another photograph.

It was a picture of a little girl in a white dress, with long fair hair, at a seaside resort, since one could see beach-huts and a section of beach and sea. 'Mara Orlov – Yalta' was written in purple ink, on the back.

'There, you see . . . the same girl . . . Gay Orlov . . . Her name was Mara . . . She didn't yet have an American first name . . . '

And he pointed to the blonde young woman in the other photo which I was still holding.

'My mother kept all these things . . . '

He rose abruptly.

'Do you mind if we stop now? My head is spinning . . . '

He passed a hand over his brow.

'I'll go and change . . . If you like, we can have dinner together . . . '

I remained alone, sitting on the floor, the photos scattered about me. I stacked them in the large red box and kept only two, which I put on the bed: the photo in which I appeared, next to Gay Orlov and the old man, Giorgiadze, and the one of Gay Orlov as a child at Yalta. I rose and went to the window.

It was night. The window looked out on to another open space with buildings round it. At the far end, the Seine, and to the left, the Pont de Puteaux. And the Île, stretching out. Lines of cars were crossing the bridge. I gazed at the façades of the buildings, all the windows lit up, just like the window at which I was standing. And in this labyrinthine maze of buildings, staircases and lifts, among these hundreds of cubbyholes, I had found a man who perhaps . . .

I had pressed my brow against the window. Below, each building entrance was lit by a yellow light which would burn all night.

'The restaurant is quite close,' he said.

I took the two photos I had left on the bed.

'Mr de Dzhagorev,' I said, 'would you be so kind as to lend me these two photos?'

'You can keep them.'

He pointed to the red box.

'You can keep all the photos.'

'But . . . I . . . '

'Take them.'

His tone was so peremptory that it was impossible to argue. When we left the apartment, I was carrying the large box under my arm.

At street level, we proceeded along the Quai du Général-Koenig.

We descended some stone steps, and there, right by the side of the Seine, was a brick building. Above the door, a sign: 'Bar-Restaurant de l'Île.' We went in. A low-ceilinged room, and tables with white paper napkins and wicker chairs. Through the windows one could see the Seine and the lights of the Pont de Puteaux. We sat down at the back of the room. We were the only customers.

Styoppa groped in his pocket and placed in the centre of the table the package I had seen him buy at the grocer's.

'The usual?' asked the waiter.

'The usual.'

'And you, sir?' asked the waiter, turning to me.

'This gentleman will have the same as me.'

Very swiftly the waiter brought us two servings of Baltic herring and poured some mineral water into two thimble-sized glasses. Styoppa extracted some cucumbers from the package in the centre of the table and we shared them.

'Is this all right for you?' he asked me.

'Do you really not wish to keep all these souvenirs?' I asked him.

'No. They're yours now. I'm handing on the torch.'

We ate in silence. A boat passed, so close, that I had time to see its occupants, framed in the window, sitting at a table and eating, just like us.

'And this . . . Gay Orlov?' I said. 'Do you know what became of her?'

'Gay Orlov? I believe she's dead.'

'Dead?'

'I believe so. I must have met her two or three times. I hardly knew her . . . It was my mother who was a friend of old Giorgiadze. A little cucumber?'

'Thanks.'

'I think she led a very restless life in America . . . '

'And you don't know anyone who could give me any information about this . . . Gay Orlov?'

He threw me a compassionate look.

'My poor friend . . . no one . . . Perhaps there's someone in America . . . '

Another boat passed, black, slow, as though abandoned.

'I always have a banana for dessert,' he said. 'What would you like?'

'I'll have one too.'

We ate our bananas.

'And Gay Orlov's . . . parents?' I asked.

'They must have died in America. One dies everywhere, you know . . . '

'Did Giorgiadze have any other relatives in France?'

He shrugged his shoulders.

'But why are you so concerned about Gay Orlov? Was she your sister?'

He smiled pleasantly.

'Some coffee?' he asked.

'No, thanks.'

'I won't either.'

He wanted to pay the bill, but I forestalled him. We left the restaurant 'de l'Île' and he took my arm as we climbed the steps of the quay. A fog had come up, soft but with an icy feel to it. It filled your lungs with such cold that you felt you were floating on air. On the quay again, I could barely make out the buildings a few yards off.

I guided him, as if he were a blind man, to his apartment building, with the staircase entrances yellow blotches in the fog, the only reference points. He clasped my hand.

'Try to find Gay Orlov even so,' he said. 'Since it means so much to you . . . '

I watched him entering the lighted entrance hall. He stopped and waved to me. I stood, motionless, the large red box under my arms, like a child returning from a birthday party, and I felt certain at that moment that he was saying something else to me but that the fog was muffling the sound of his voice.

5

A postcard showing the Promenade des Anglais. Summertime.

My dear Guy, your letter arrived safely. Here, every day

is like the next, but Nice is a very lovely town. You must come and visit me. Strangely enough, I run into people on the street I have not seen for thirty years, or who I thought were dead. We give each other quite a turn. Nice is a city of ghosts and spectres, but I hope not to become one of them right away.

As to the woman you are looking for, the best thing would be to phone Bernardy, Mac Mahon 00-08. He has kept in close contact with people in the various departments. He will be happy to advise you.

Hoping to see you in Nice, my dear Guy, I remain yours most sincerely and affectionately,

Hutte

P.S. As you know, the premises of the Agency are at your disposal.

6

23rd October 1965

Subject: ORLOV, Mara, called 'Gay' ORLOV.

Born in: Moscow (Russia), in 1914, daughter of Kyril ORLOV and Irene GIORGIADZE.

Nationality: stateless. (Miss Orlov's parents and she herself, as Russian refugees, were not recognized by the Government of the Union of Soviet Socialist Republics as its nationals.) Miss Orlov had an ordinary residence permit. Miss Orlov evidently arrived in France, in 1936, from the United States. In the U.S.A. she entered into marriage with a Mr Waldo Blunt, then divorced.

Miss Orlov resided successively at:

The Hôtel Chateaubriand, 18 Rue du Cirque, Paris 8
53 Avenue Montaigne, Paris 8

Before coming to France, Miss Orlov was a dancer in the
United States. In Paris, there was no visible source of
income, although she led a life of luxury.

Miss Orlov died in 1950 at her home, 25 Avenue du
Maréchal-Lyautey, Paris 16, of an overdose of bar-
biturates.

Mr Waldo Blunt, her ex-husband, has resided in Paris
since 1952 and has worked in various night club
establishments as a professional pianist. He is an
American citizen. Born 30th September 1910, in
Chicago.

Residence permit no. 534HC828.

Attached to this typewritten memorandum, a visiting-
card bearing Jean-Pierre Bernardy's name and the
words:

'This is all the information available. My best wishes.
Regards to Hutte.'

7

A notice on the glass fronted door announced, 'Waldo
Blunt at the piano from six to nine every evening in the
Hilton Hotel bar.'

The bar was packed and the only free seat was at the
table of a Japanese with gold-rimmed spectacles. He did
not seem to understand me when I bent over him and
asked if I might sit down, and when I did, he took no
notice.

American and Japanese customers came in, hailed
each other and spoke louder and louder. They stood
about between the tables. Several, glass in hand, leant
on the backs or arms of chairs. One young woman was
even perched on the knees of a grey-haired man.

Waldo Blunt arrived a quarter of an hour late and sat down at the piano. A small plump man with receding hair and a thin moustache. He was wearing a grey suit. First he turned his head and cast a glance around the tables where people were crowding. He stroked the keys of the piano with his right hand and played a few random chords. I happened to be sitting at one of the closest tables.

He began a tune which, I believe, was 'Sur les quais du vieux Paris', but the noise of conversation and the bursts of laughter made the music barely audible, and even close to the piano, I could not catch all the notes. He continued imperturbably, sitting bolt upright, his head bent. I felt sorry for him: I supposed that at one time in his life he had been listened to when he played the piano. Since then, he must have got used to this perpetual buzz, drowning out his music. What would he say, when I mentioned Gay Orlov's name? Would it temporarily jolt him out of the apathetic state in which he played? Or would it no longer mean anything to him, like these notes, unable to still the hum of conversation?

The bar had gradually emptied. The only ones left now were the Japanese with the gold-rimmed spectacles, myself, and at the back of the room, the young woman I had seen perched on the lap of the grey-haired gentleman and who was now seated next to a fat, red-faced man in a light blue suit . . . They were speaking German. And very loudly. Waldo Blunt was playing a slow tune which I knew well.

He turned towards us.

'Would you like me to play anything in particular, ladies and gentlemen?' he asked in a cold voice with a trace of an American accent.

The Japanese next to me did not react. He remained motionless, his face smooth, and I was afraid he might topple from his seat at the slightest breath of air, since he was clearly an embalmed corpse.

' "Sag warum", please,' the woman huskily called from the back.

Blunt gave a slight nod and started playing 'Sag warum'. The light in the bar dimmed, as it sometimes does in dance halls at the first notes of a slow step. The couple took the opportunity to kiss and the woman's hand slid into the opening of the fat, red-faced man's shirt, then lower down. The gold-rimmed spectacles of the Japanese flashed. At his piano, Blunt looked like an automaton being jolted spasmodically: 'Sag warum' requires an endless thumping out of chords.

What was he thinking about? Behind him, a fat, red-faced man stroked a blonde's thigh and an embalmed Japanese had been sitting in his chair in the Hilton bar for several days. I was sure he was thinking about nothing. He was enveloped in a fog of indifference that grew thicker and thicker. Did I have the right to rouse him from it, to force him to think of something painful?

The fat, red-faced man and the blonde left the bar, no doubt to take a room. The man was pulling her by the arm and she almost stumbled. The Japanese and I were the only ones left.

Blunt again turned to us and said in his cold voice:

'Would you like me to play something else?'

The Japanese made no movement.

' "Que reste-t-il de nos amours", please,' I said.

He played the tune in a strangely slow manner, and the melody seemed drawn out, trapped in a swamp from which the notes had trouble freeing themselves. From time to time he paused, like an exhausted walker who staggers a little. He looked at his watch, rose abruptly, and inclined his head for our benefit:

'Gentlemen, it is 9 o'clock. Good night.'

He left. I fell into step behind him, leaving the embalmed Japanese in the crypt of the bar.

He walked down the corridor and crossed the deserted lounge.

I caught up with him.

'Mr Waldo Blunt? . . . I would like to speak to you.'

'What about?'

He threw me a hunted look.

'About someone you used to know . . . A woman called Gay. Gay Orlov . . . '

He stopped short in the middle of the lounge.

'Gay . . . '

He stared as though the light of a projector had been turned on his face.

'You . . . you knew . . . Gay?'

'No.'

We had left the hotel. There was a line of men and women in gaudy evening attire – long, green or pale-blue, satin dresses, and garnet-coloured dinner-jackets – waiting for taxis.

'I don't want to trouble you . . . '

'You're not troubling me,' he said in a preoccupied tone. 'It's such a long time since I've heard Gay mentioned . . . But who are you?'

'A cousin of hers. I . . . I'd like to find out a few things about her . . . '

'A few things?'

He rubbed his temple with his forefinger.

'What do you want to know?'

We had turned into a narrow street which ran along-side the hotel and led to the Seine.

'I must be getting home,' he said.

'I'll walk with you.'

'So, you're Gay's cousin, really?'

'Yes. The family would like some information about her.'

'She's been dead a long time.'

'I know.'

He was walking at a rapid pace and I had trouble keeping up with him. I tried to stay on the same level as him. We had reached the Quai Branly.

'I live over there,' he said, pointing to the other bank of the Seine.

We stepped out on to the Pont Bir-Hakeim.

'I won't be able to give you much information,' he said. 'I knew Gay a very long time ago.'

He had slowed down, as if he felt safe. Perhaps he had been walking quickly until then because he thought he was being followed. Or to shake me off.

'I didn't know Gay had any family,' he said.

'Yes . . . she did . . . on the Giorgiadze side . . . '

'I beg your pardon?'

'The Giorgiadze family . . . Her grandfather was called Giorgiadze . . . '

'Oh, I see . . . '

He stopped and leant against the stone parapet of the bridge. I could not do likewise, as it made me dizzy. So, I stayed upright, standing in front of him. He seemed reluctant to speak.

'You know . . . I was married to her? . . . '

'I know.'

'How do you know?'

'It was in some old papers.'

'We were both working in a night club, in New York . . . I played the piano . . . She asked me to marry her only because she wanted to stay in America, and not have any problems with the immigration people . . . '

He shook his head at this memory.

'She was a strange girl. After that, she went with Lucky Luciano . . . She'd known him when she was working in the Palm Island casino . . . '

'Luciano?'

'Yes, yes, Luciano . . . She was with him when he was arrested, in Arkansas . . . After that, she met a Frenchman and I heard she left for France with him . . . '

His gaze lightened. He smiled at me.

'It's nice to be able to talk about Gay, you know . . . '

A Metro train passed by, overhead, in the direction of the right bank. Then a second one, going the other way. Their din drowned out Blunt's voice. He was saying something to me, I could tell by the movement of his lips.

'. . . The prettiest girl I ever knew . . .'

This scrap of speech which I managed to catch made me feel suddenly despondent. Here was I, in the middle of a bridge, at night, with a man I did not know, trying to drag some information out of him which would tell me something about myself, and I could not hear him for the noise of trains.

'Can we perhaps move on a bit?'

But he was so engrossed that he did not answer me. It was such a long time, no doubt, since he had thought about Gay Orlov, that all his memories of her were rising to the surface and making his head spin, like a sea breeze. He stayed there, leaning against the parapet of the bridge.

'I'd appreciate it if we could move on a bit.'

'Did you know Gay? Did you meet her?'

'No. That's why I need the information.'

'She was a blonde . . . with green eyes . . . A very special blonde . . . How can I describe it? An ash-blonde . . .'

An ash-blonde. And who perhaps had played an important part in my life. I would have to study her photograph carefully. And, gradually, everything would come back. Unless he gave me some better clues in the end. It was already a piece of luck to have found him, Waldo Blunt.

I took his arm, as we could not stay on the bridge. We walked along the Quai de Passy.

'Did you see her again in France?' I asked him.

'No. When I got to France, she was already dead. She committed suicide . . .'

'Why?'

'She often told me she was frightened of getting old . . .'

'When did you last see her?'

'After the business with Luciano, she met this Frenchman. We saw each other a few times in those days . . .'

'Did you know the Frenchman?'

'No. She told me she was going to marry him, to get French nationality . . . She was obsessed with getting a nationality . . . '

'But you were divorced?'

'Of course . . . Our marriage lasted six months . . . Just long enough to keep the immigration authorities quiet. They'd wanted to expel her from the States . . . '

I had to concentrate, so as not to lose track of his story. Especially as he had a very soft voice.

'She left for France . . . And I never saw her again . . . Until I learnt . . . her suicide . . . '

'How did you find out?'

'Through an American friend who had known Gay and who was in Paris at the time. He sent me a small cutting from a paper . . . '

'Did you keep it?'

'Yes. It must be at my place, in a drawer.'

We were approaching the Trocadero Gardens. The fountains were illuminated and there was a lot of traffic. Tourists had gathered in groups in front of the fountains and on the Pont d'Iéna. A Saturday evening in October, but because of the warmth of the air, the pedestrians, and the trees which had still not lost their leaves, it felt like a springtime weekend.

'I live a bit further on . . . '

We passed the Gardens and had turned down the Avenue de New-York. There, under the embankment trees, I had the unpleasant sensation that I was dreaming. I had already lived my life and was just a ghost hovering in the tepid air of a Saturday evening. Why try to renew ties which had been broken and look for paths that had been blocked off long ago? And this plump, moustachioed little man, walking beside me, hardly seemed real.

'It's funny, I've suddenly remembered the name of the Frenchman Gay knew in America . . . '

42

'What was it?' I asked unsteadily.

'Howard . . . That was his surname . . . not his Christian name . . . Just a moment . . . Howard de something . . . '

I stopped and leant closer to him.

'Howard de what?'

'De . . . de . . . de Luz. L . . . U . . . Z . . . Howard de Luz . . . '

Howard de Luz . . . the name was striking . . . half English . . . half French . . . or Spanish . . .

'And his first name?'

'I don't know . . . '

He made a helpless gesture.

'You don't know what he looked like, physically?'

'No.'

I would show him the photo of Gay, old Giorgiadze, and the one I thought was myself.

'And what did this Howard de Luz do?'

'Gay told me he belonged to a noble family . . . He did nothing.'

He gave a short laugh.

'Ah, yes . . . just a moment . . . It's coming back to me . . . He'd spent a lot of time in Hollywood . . . And there, Gay told me, he was the confidant of the actor, John Gilbert . . . '

'John Gilbert's confidant?'

'Yes . . . Towards the end of Gilbert's life . . . '

Traffic on the Avenue de New-York was moving fast but made no sound you could hear, and this increased the dream-like feeling. Cars flowed along in a muffled, fluid world, as though skimming over water. We reached the foot-bridge, before the Pont d'Alma. Howard de Luz. It might be my own name. Howard de Luz. Yes, the sound of it stirred something in me, something as fleeting as moonlight passing over some object. If I was this Howard de Luz, I had shown a certain originality in my life style, since, among so many more reputable and absorbing professions, I had

43

chosen that of being John Gilbert's confidant.

Just before we reached the Museum of Modern Art, we turned down a narrow street.

'Here's where I live,' he said.

The lift light did not work and the automatic time-switch light went out just as we started on our way up. In the dark, we heard laughter and music.

The lift stopped, and I could feel Blunt, next to me, trying to find the handle of the landing gate. He opened it and I jostled him leaving the lift, as it was pitch dark. The laughter and music came from the floor we were on. Blunt turned a key in a lock.

He left the door ajar behind us and we were in the middle of an entrance hall, weakly lit by a bare bulb hanging from the ceiling. Blunt stood there, non-plussed. I wondered if I hadn't better take my leave. The music was deafening. Coming from inside the apartment, a young red-haired woman in a red bathing-wrap appeared. She considered us both, eyes wide with astonishment. The very loosely fitting wrap revealed her breasts.

'My wife,' said Blunt.

She gave me a slight nod and with both hands drew the collar of the wrap closer.

'I didn't know you were coming back so early,' she said.

All three of us stood there, without moving, under the light which cast a pallid glow over our faces, and I turned to Blunt.

'You could have warned me,' he said to her.

'I didn't know . . . '

A child caught out telling lies. She lowered her head. The deafening music had stopped and a tune, played on the saxophone, followed, so pure it melted into the air.

'Are there many?' asked Blunt.

'No, no . . . a few friends . . . '

A head appeared in the narrow opening of the door, a blonde with very short hair and pale, almost pink lipstick. Then another head, dark hair, dull complexion. The light from the bulb gave these faces the look of masks, and the dark-haired woman smiled.

'I must return to my friends . . . Come back in two or three hours . . . '

'All right,' said Blunt.

She left the entrance-hall preceded by the two others and shut the door. Bursts of laughter and the sound of a chase could be heard. Then, the deafening music again.

'Come on!' said Blunt.

Once again we were on the staircase landing. Blunt pressed the automatic time-switch and sat down on a step. He motioned to me to sit down beside him.

'My wife's a lot younger than me . . . thirty years difference . . . You should never marry a woman a lot younger than you . . . Never . . . '

He had laid a hand on my shoulder.

'It never works . . . There's not a single case of its working . . . Remember that, old chap . . . '

The light went out. Blunt evidently had no wish to switch it on again. Neither did I, for that matter.

'If Gay could see me . . . '

He burst out laughing at the thought. Strange laughter, in the dark.

'She wouldn't know me . . . I've put on nearly five stones, since . . . '

A burst of laughter, but different from the first one, more tense, strained.

'She'd be very disappointed . . . Think of it. A bar room pianist . . . '

'But why disappointed?'

'And in a month, I'll be out of work . . . '

He gripped my arm, round the biceps.

'Gay thought I was going to be the new Cole Porter . . . '

Female screams, suddenly. It came from Blunt's apartment.

'What's going on?' I said.

'Nothing, they're enjoying themselves.'

A man's voice bellowing: 'Are you going to let me in? Are you going to let me in, Dany?' Laughter. A door slamming.

'Dany's my wife,' whispered Blunt.

He rose and switched on the light.

'Let's get a breath of air.'

We crossed the esplanade of the Museum of Modern Art and sat down on the steps. I watched the cars, further down, moving along the Avenue de New-York, the only sign of life. Everything about us was deserted, frozen. Even the Eiffel Tower, which I could make out on the other side of the Seine, the Eiffel Tower generally so reassuring, looked like a hulk of oxidized scrap-iron.

'You can breathe here,' said Blunt.

And indeed a warm breeze was playing over the esplanade, among the statues which looked like shadowy blotches, and the big columns at the far end.

'I'd like to show you some photographs,' I said to Blunt.

I took an envelope from my pocket, opened it and drew out two photographs: the one of Gay Orlov, with old Giorgiadze and the man I believed to be myself, and the one of her as a little girl. I handed him the first photograph.

'Can't see anything here,' muttered Blunt.

He flicked a cigarette-lighter but had to try several times, as the wind kept blowing out the flame. He shielded it with the palm of his hand and moved the lighter closer to the photograph.

'Do you see that man?' I said. 'On the left . . . The extreme left . . . '

'Yes.'

'Do you know him?'

'No.'

He was bent over the photograph, his hand like an eye-shade against his forehead, to shield the flame.

'Don't you think he looks like me?'

'I don't know.'

He scrutinized the photograph for another few seconds and handed it back to me.

'Gay was just like that when I knew her,' he said sadly.

'Here, this is one of her as a child.'

I handed him the other photograph and he examined it by the lighter flame, his hand still shielding it, pressed against his forehead, looking like a watchmaker engaged in a particularly delicate operation.

'She was a pretty little girl,' he said. 'Have you any other photos of her?'

'Unfortunately not . . . Have you?'

'I had a photograph of our wedding, but I lost it in America . . . I even wonder if I've kept the newspaper cutting of her suicide . . . '

His American accent, which had been imperceptible at first, was growing stronger and stronger. Fatigue?

'Do you often have to wait like this, before you can go home?'

'More and more. And yet it all started so well . . . My wife used to be very nice . . . '

He lit a cigarette with difficulty, because of the wind.

'Gay would be amazed if she saw me like this . . . '

He drew closer to me and laid a hand on my shoulder.

'She had the right idea, old man, don't you think – to disappear before it gets too late?'

I looked at him. Everything about him was round. His face, his blue eyes and even the thin moustache, cut in an arc. His mouth too, and his plump and dimpled hands. He made me think of those balloons children hold on a string and which they sometimes release to see how high they will climb. And the name, Waldo Blunt, bulged, like one of those balloons.

'I'm dreadfully sorry I haven't been able to tell you much about Gay, old man . . . '

I could sense him weighed down with fatigue,

dejected, and yet I watched him very closely for fear that a puff of wind across the esplanade might carry him off, leaving me alone with my questions.

8

The avenue skirts the Auteuil race-course. On one side, a ride, on the other blocks of flats all built on the same pattern with open spaces between. I passed in front of these de-luxe barracks and took up a position facing the one where Gay Orlov committed suicide: 25, Avenue du Maréchal-Lyautey. Which floor? The caretaker would certainly have changed since then. Was there still anyone living in the building who would have run into Gay Orlov on the stairs, or who took the lift with her? Or who would recognize me, as a frequent visitor?

There must have been evenings when I climbed the stairs of 25, Avenue du Maréchal-Lyautey, my heart thumping. She was waiting for me. Her windows looked out on to the race-course. It must have been strange to see the races from up there, the horses and their tiny jockeys, like the procession of little figures moving across the end of a shooting-gallery and if you knocked them all down, you won the big prize.

In what language did we speak to each other? English? Had the photo with old Giorgiadze been taken in this apartment? How was it furnished? What could they have had to say to each other, this Howard de Luz – me? – of 'a noble family' and the 'confidant of John Gilbert', and a former dancer, born in Moscow, who had known Lucky Luciano in Palm Island?

Strange people. The kind that leave the merest blur behind them, soon vanished. Hutte and I often used to talk about these traceless beings. They spring up out of nothing one fine day and return there, having sparkled a little. Beauty queens. Gigolos. Butterflies. Most of them, even when alive, had no more substance than steam which will never condense. Hutte, for instance, used to quote the case of a fellow he called 'the beach man'. This man had spent forty years of his life on beaches or by the sides of swimming pools, chatting pleasantly with summer visitors and rich idlers. He is to be seen, in his bathing costume, in the corners and backgrounds of thousands of holiday snaps, among groups of happy people, but no one knew his name and why he was there. And no one noticed when one day he vanished from the photographs. I did not dare tell Hutte, but I felt that 'the beach man' was myself. Though it would not have surprised him if I had confessed it. Hutte was always saying that, in the end, we were all 'beach men' and that 'the sand' – I am quoting his own words – 'keeps the traces of our foot-steps only a few moments.'

On one side, the building faced an open space that seemed deserted. A large clump of trees, bushes, a lawn which had not been cut for a long time. A child was playing there alone, quietly, in front of a mound of sand, on this sunny late afternoon. I sat down by the lawn and lifted my head towards the building, wondering if Gay Orlov's windows looked out on this side.

9

It is night and the opaline light in the Agency is reflected in the leather top of Hutte's desk. I am seated at this desk. I am going through old street-and-trade directories, more recent ones, and noting down what I find as I go along: HOWARD DE LUZ (Jean Simety) ✠ and Mme, born MABEL DONAHUE at Valbreuse, Orne. T. 21 and 23, Rue Raynouard, T. AUT 15–28.

$-$ CGP $-$ MA ⚓

The social directory where this is to be found goes back thirty years. Does it refer to my father?

The same reference in successive directories. I look up the list of signs and abbreviations.

✠ means: Military Cross.

CGP: Club du Grand Pavois, MA: Motor Yacht Club of the Côte d'Azur, and ⚓ : owner of sailing vessel.

But ten years later the following disappear: 23, Rue Raynouard T. AUT 15–28. Also: MA and ⚓ .

The following year, all that remains is: HOWARD DE LUZ, Mme, born MABEL DONAHUE at Valbreuse, Orne. T. 21.

Then nothing at all.

Next, I consult the Parisian year-books of the last ten years. Each time, Howard de Luz's name appears in the following form:

HOWARD DE LUZ C. 3 Square Henri-Paté. 16 – MOL 50–52. A brother? Cousin?

No reference to him in the social directories of the same years.

10

'Mr Howard is expecting you.'

No doubt the proprietress of this restaurant in the Rue de Bassano: dark hair, pale eyes. She motioned to me to follow her, we went down some stairs and she led me towards the back of the room. She stopped in front of a table where a man was sitting on his own. He rose.

'Claude Howard,' he said.

He motioned to the chair opposite. We sat down.

'I'm late. Forgive me.'

'Not at all.'

He stared at me with curiosity. Did he recognize me?

'Your telephone call intrigued me a great deal,' he said.

I tried to smile.

'And particularly your interest in the Howard de Luz family . . . of which I am, my dear sir, the last representative . . . '

He had spoken these words in an ironic, self-mocking tone of voice.

'Besides, I call myself Howard, quite simply. It's less complicated.'

He handed me the menu.

'You don't have to order the same as I do. I'm a gastronomical columnist . . . I have to try the house specialities . . . sweetbread and the fish bouillon . . . '

He sighed. He really seemed to be at a low ebb.

'I've had enough of it . . . Whatever's going on in my life, I'm always obliged to eat . . . '

They were already bringing him some meat pie. I ordered salad and a fruit.

'You're lucky . . . I have to eat . . . I have to write my piece this evening. I've just returned from the Golden Tripe Competition . . . I was one of the judges. We had to swallow a hundred and seventy pieces of tripe over a period of one and a half days . . . '

I could not tell his age. His hair, which was very dark, was brushed backwards, his eyes were brown, and there was something negroid about his features, in spite of the extreme pallor of his complexion. We were alone at the back of this section of the restaurant, in the basement, with its decor of pale blue panelling, satin, and crystal wear, all of which gave it a kind of gimcrack eighteenth-century air.

51

'I've been thinking about what you told me on the telephone . . . The Howard de Luz you're interested in can only be my cousin Freddie . . . '

'You really think so?'

'I'm sure of it. But I hardly knew him . . . '

'Freddie Howard de Luz?'

'Yes. We played together a few times when we were little.'

'Have you a photo of him?'

'Not one.'

He swallowed a mouthful of meat pie and suppressed a heave of the stomach.

'He wasn't even a first cousin . . . but once or twice removed . . . There were very few Howard de Luz's . . . I believe we were the only ones, dad and I, and Freddie and his grandfather . . . It's a French family from Mauritius, you see . . . '

He pushed away his plate with a weary gesture.

'Freddie's grandfather had married an extremely wealthy American woman . . . '

'Mabel Donahue?'

'That's the name . . . They had a magnificent estate in the Orne district . . . '

'In Valbreuse?'

'My dear fellow, you're a veritable mine.'

He threw me an astonished look.

'And then afterwards, I think they lost everything . . . Freddie went to America . . . I can't give you any more precise information . . . I only know this from hearsay . . . I don't even know if Freddie is still alive . . . '

'How could one find out?'

'If my father were here . . . I used to get news of the family from him . . . Unfortunately . . . '

I took the photo of Gay Orlov and old Giorgiadze out of my pocket and pointed to the dark-haired man who looked like me:

'Do you know this fellow?'

'No.'

'Don't you think he looks like me?'

He bent over the photograph.

'Perhaps,' he said without conviction.

'And the blonde woman, do you know her?'

'No.'

'And yet she was a friend of your cousin Freddie.'

He seemed to suddenly remember something.

'Just a moment . . . it's coming back to me . . . Freddie went to America. And it seems that there he became the actor, John Gilbert's confidant . . . '

John Gilbert's confidant. This was the second time I was being given this piece of information, but it did not lead anywhere in particular.

'I know, because he sent me a postcard from America at the time . . . '

'Did you keep it?'

'No, but I still remember what it said by heart: "Everything fine. America is a beautiful country. I've found work: I'm John Gilbert's confidant. Regards to you and your father. Freddie." It made an impression on me . . . '

'You didn't see him, when he returned to France?'

'No. I didn't even know that he had returned to France.'

'And if he were sitting opposite you now, would you recognize him?'

'Maybe not.'

I did not dare suggest to him that Freddie Howard de Luz was myself. I did not yet have formal proof of that, but I was full of hope.

'The Freddie I knew was ten years old . . . my father took me along to Valbreuse to play with him . . . '

The wine-waiter had stopped at our table and was waiting for Claude Howard to make his choice, but the latter did not notice his presence and the man stood there very stiff, looking like a sentry.

'To tell you the truth, I think Freddie is dead . . . '

'You shouldn't say that . . . '

'It's kind of you to take an interest in our unfortunate family. We didn't have much luck . . . I think I'm the sole survivor and look what I have to do to earn my living . . . '

He banged his fist on the table, while waiters brought the fish bouillon and the proprietress of the restaurant came up with an ingratiating smile.

'Mr Howard . . . Did the Golden Tripe go well this year?'

But he had not heard and leant towards me.

'Really,' he said, 'we should never have left Mauritius . . . '

II

A little old railway station, yellow and grey, with elaborate cement barriers on either side, and beyond these barriers the platform on to which I disembarked from the rail-car. The station square was deserted except for a child roller-skating under the trees on the raised strip.

I've played there too, I thought, a long time ago. This quiet place really did remind me of something. My grandfather, Howard de Luz, used to meet me on the Paris train or was it the other way round? On summer evenings, I used to wait on the station platform accompanied by my grandmother, born Mabel Donahue.

A little further, a road wide as an autoroute, but with very few cars passing. I skirted some public gardens surrounded by the same cement walls I had seen on the station square.

On the other side of the street, shops under a kind of

awning. A cinema. Then an inn, hidden among trees, at the corner of a gently ascending avenue. I stepped out unhesitatingly, as I had studied the map of Valbreuse. At the end of this tree-lined avenue, a surrounding wall and an iron gate on which was a rotting board with the half-obliterated words: ESTATE MANAGEMENT. Beyond the gate stretched a neglected lawn. At the far end, a long brick and stone structure, in the style of Louis XIII. In the middle, a pavilion, one storey higher, stood out, and the façade was completed at either end by two side pavilions with cupolas. The shutters of all the windows were closed.

A feeling of desolation swept over me: I was, perhaps, standing before the château where I had spent my childhood. I pushed the iron gate and it opened without difficulty. How long had it been since I had crossed its threshold? To the right, I noticed a brick building which had to be the stables.

The grass reached to mid-calf and I crossed the lawn as quickly as I could, walking towards the château. This silent structure intrigued me. I was afraid I would find that behind the façade there was nothing but tall grass and sections of crumbling masonry.

Someone called to me. I turned round. Over by the stable buildings, a man was waving his arm. He walked towards me and I stood still, in the middle of the lawn which looked like a jungle, watching him. A rather tall, heavily built man, dressed in green velvet.

'What do you want?'

He had stopped a few paces from me. Dark-haired, with a moustache.

'I would like some information about Mr Howard de Luz.'

I stepped forward. Perhaps he would recognize me? Each time, I have the same hope, and each time I am disappointed.

'Which Mr Howard de Luz?'

'Freddie.'

I said 'Freddie' in a different tone of voice, as if it was my own name I was throwing out, after years of having forgotten it.

He stared.

'Freddie . . . '

At that moment, I really believed he was addressing me by my first name.

'Freddie? But he's no longer here . . . '

No, he had not recognized me. No one recognized me.

'What is it that you want exactly?'

'I'd like to know what became of Freddie Howard de Luz . . . '

He stared at me suspiciously and thrust a hand into his trouser pocket. He was going to bring out a gun and threaten me. No. He pulled a handkerchief from his pocket and mopped his brow.

'Who are you?'

'I knew Freddie in America a long time ago, and I'd like some news of him.'

His face brightened up suddenly at this lie.

'In America? You knew Freddie in America?'

The word 'America' seemed to send him into a reverie. He was so grateful to me for having known Freddie 'in America', he seemed ready to embrace me.

'In America? So, you knew him when he was, when he was . . . '

'John Gilbert's confidant.'

All his suspicions melted away.

He even took me by the hand.

'Come this way.'

He led me to the left, skirting the surrounding wall, where the grass was less tall and one could just make out an old path.

'I've had no news of Freddie for a long time,' he said in a solemn voice.

His green velvet suit was worn right down in places, and pieces of leather had been sewn on to the shoulders, elbows and knees.

'Are you American?'

'Yes.'

'Freddie sent me several postcards from America.'

'Did you keep them?'

'Of course.'

We walked towards the château.

'You've never been here?' he asked me.

'Never.'

'But how did you get the address?'

'Through a cousin of Freddie's, Claude Howard de Luz . . .'

'I don't know him.'

We approached one of the cupola-topped pavilions I had noticed at either end of the château's façade. We skirted it. He pointed to a small door:

'It's the only door you can get in by.'

He turned a key in the lock. We entered. He led me through a dark, empty room, then along a corridor. We came out into another room, with stained glass windows which made it look like a chapel or a winter garden.

'This was the summer dining-room,' he said.

No furniture, except for an old divan, covered in worn red velvet upholstery on which we sat. He took a pipe from his pocket and lit it calmly. The stained glass windows gave the daylight that filtered through a pale blue tint.

I lifted my head and noticed that the ceiling too was pale blue, with brighter patches – clouds. He had followed my look.

'Freddie painted the ceiling and wall.'

The only wall in the room was painted green and one could see a palm-tree that had almost faded away. I tried to imagine this room as it had been, when we used to have our meals here. The ceiling where I had painted the sky. The green wall, with its palm-tree, by which I had hoped to lend the room a tropical air. The stained glass windows through which blue-tinted daylight fell on our faces. But whose faces?

'This is the only room one can still get into,' he said. 'All the others are under seal.'

'Why?'

'The house is sequestrated.'

These words sent a chill through me.

'They've sequestrated everything, but they've left me here. How long, I don't know.'

He pulled on his pipe and shook his head.

'From time to time, some fellow from the Estate takes a look around. They don't seem to be able to make up their minds.'

'Who?'

'The Estate.'

I did not quite understand what he meant, but I remembered the rotting wooden signboard: 'Estate Management.'

'Have you been here long?'

'Oh, yes . . . I came when Mr Howard de Luz died . . . Freddie's grandfather . . . I looked after the grounds and was the mistress's chauffeur . . . Freddie's grandmother . . . '

'And Freddie's parents?'

'I think they died very young. He was raised by his grandparents.'

So, I had been raised by my grandparents. After the death of my grandfather, I lived here alone, with my grandmother, born Mabel Donahue, and this man.

'What's your name?' I asked him.

'Robert.'

'What did Freddie call you?'

'His grandmother called me Bob. She was American. Freddie called me Bob too.'

The name Bob meant nothing to me. But, then, he did not recognize me either.

'Then, the grandmother died. Things weren't going too well financially by then . . . Freddie's grandfather had squandered his wife's fortune . . . A very big American fortune . . . '

He pulled sedately on his pipe and thin streams of blue smoke rose to the ceiling. This room with its large stained glass windows and Freddie's – my? – decorations on the wall and ceiling was obviously a haven for him.

'Then Freddie disappeared . . . Without any warning . . . I don't know what happened. But the lot was sequestrated.'

Again the term 'sequestrated', like a door slamming in my face just as I was about to cross its threshold.

'And since then, I've been waiting . . . I wonder what they intend doing about me . . . They can't throw me out after all.'

'Where do you live?'

'In the old stables. Freddie's grandfather had them fitted out.'

He studied me, his pipe clenched between his teeth.

'And how about you? Tell me how you got to know Freddie in America.'

'Oh . . . It's a long story . . . '

'Would you like to take a walk? I'll show you the grounds on that side.'

'With pleasure.'

He opened the french windows and we went down some stone steps. We were standing before a lawn like the one I had tried to cross to reach the château, but here, the grass was not nearly so high. To my astonishment, the back of the château did not conform at all with its façade: it was built of grey stone. The roof was not the same either: on this side it was more elaborate, with cut off corners and gables, so that a house which at first sight looked like a Louis XIII château, from the back looked like one of those late-nineteenth-century seaside resort mansions, a few rare specimens of which still survive in Biarritz.

'I try to keep up the whole of this side of the park a bit,' he said. 'But it's not easy for a man on his own.'

We were following a gravel path which skirted the lawn. The bushes on our left, head-high, were carefully trimmed. He motioned towards them:

'The maze. It was planted by Freddie's grandfather. I do the best I can with it. After all, something ought to stay the way it was.'

We entered the 'maze' by one of its side-entrances, stooping because of the greenery which met overhead. Several of the paths intersected, there were cross-roads, circuses, circular and right-angle bends, dead-ends, an arbour with a green bench . . . As a child, I must have played games of hide-and-seek here with my grandfather or with friends of my own age. In this enchanted place, which smelt of privet and pine, I must surely have known the best moments of my life. When we left the maze, I could not resist saying to my guide:

'It's odd . . . It reminds me of something . . . '

But he did not seem to hear me.

At the edge of the lawn, a rusty old frame from which hung two swings.

'Would you mind if we . . . '

He sat down on one of the swings and lit his pipe again. I seated myself on the other. The sun was setting and bathed the lawn and bushes of the maze in a delicate orange glow. And the grey stone of the château was speckled in the same way.

I chose this moment to hand him the photo of Gay Orlov, old Giorgiadze and myself.

'Do you know these people?'

He studied the photo for a long time, without taking the pipe from his mouth.

'I knew that one, all right . . . '

He put his forefinger over Gay Orlov's face.

'The Russian woman . . . '

He said this in a musing tone, smiling.

'Yes, I certainly knew the Russian woman . . . '

He gave a short laugh.

'Freddie often brought her here in the last few years

. . . Some girl . . . A blonde . . . She really knew how to drink, I can tell you . . . Did you know her?'

'Yes,' I said. 'I met her with Freddie in America.'

'He knew the Russian woman in America, did he?'

'Yes.'

'She could tell you where Freddie is right now . . . You should ask her . . . '

'And this dark-haired fellow, here, next to the Russian?'

He leant a bit closer to the photo and scrutinized it. My heart was thumping.

'Yes . . . I knew him too . . . Just a moment . . . Yes, of course . . . He was a friend of Freddie's . . . He used to come here with Freddie, the Russian woman and another girl . . . I think he was a South American or something like that . . . '

'Don't you think he looks like me?'

'Yes . . . Could be,' he said without conviction.

So, it was clear my name was not Freddie Howard de Luz. I looked at the lawn with its high grass whose borders caught the last rays of the setting sun. I had never walked this lawn, arm in arm with an American grandmother. I had never played, as a child, in this 'maze'. The frame, with its swings, had not been put up for me. Pity.

'You say, South American?'

'Yes . . . But he spoke French like you and me . . . '

'And you often saw him here?'

'A few times.'

'How did you know he was South American?'

'Because one day I went to Paris to fetch him by car and bring him back here. He'd told me to pick him up at the place where he worked . . . A South American embassy . . . '

'Which embassy?'

'There you're asking too much . . . '

The change in my circumstances took some getting used to. I was no longer the scion of a family whose

61

name appeared in a number of old social directories and even in the year-book, but a South American whose trail would be infinitely harder to pick up.

'I think he was a childhood friend of Freddie's . . . '

'He came here with a woman?'

'Yes. Two or three times. A Frenchwoman. The four of them used to come here together . . . After the grandmother's death . . . '

He rose.

'Shall we go in? It's getting cold . . . '

Night had almost fallen and once again we found ourselves in the 'summer dining-room'.

'This was Freddie's favourite room . . . All four of them, Freddie, the Russian woman, the South American and the other girl, used to sit up here very late in the evening . . . '

The divan was no more than a soft blur and a lattice work of shadows danced on the ceiling in diamond shapes. I tried in vain to recapture the echoes of our evenings together.

'They put a billiard-table in here . . . The South American's girlfriend was the one who particularly liked billiards . . . She won every time . . . I can tell you because I played her several times . . . The table's still here, by the way . . . '

He led me into a dark corridor, switching on an electric torch, and we emerged into a tiled hall with a majestic staircase sweeping up from it.

'The main entrance . . . '

Under the stairs, there was, indeed, a billiard-table. He shone his torch on it. A white ball, in the centre, as though the game had been interrupted and would start again at any moment. And as though Gay Orlov, or I, or Freddie, or the mysterious Frenchwoman who accompanied me here, or Bob, were already leaning forward, to take aim.

'You see, the billiard-table's still there . . . '

He swept the majestic staircase with his torch.

'It's no use going up to the other floors . . . The whole lot's under seal . . . '

I thought – Freddie had a room up there. A child's room, then a young man's room with bookshelves, photographs on the wall, and – who knows? – perhaps one of them showing all four of us, or the two of us, Freddie and me, arm in arm. He leant against the billiard-table to re-light his pipe. I, for my part, could not help staring at this great staircase which it was no use climbing, because up there, everything was 'under seal'.

We left by the small side door, which he closed, turning the key twice in the lock. It was dark.

'I've got to catch the train to Paris,' I told him.

'Come with me.'

He gripped my arm and we followed the surrounding wall until we reached the old stables. He opened a glass-fronted door and lit an oil lamp.

'They cut off the electricity ages ago . . . But they forgot to cut the water . . . '

We were in a room, in the middle of which was a dark, wooden table and some wicker chairs. On the walls, earthenware plates and some copper dishes. A stuffed boar's head over the window.

'I'm going to give you something.'

He crossed the room to a cupboard at the other end, and opened it. He took out a box which he placed on the table, with the words 'Biscuits Lefebvre Utile – Nantes' on its lid. Then he stood in front of me.

'You were a friend of Freddie's, weren't you?' he said in a voice full of feeling.

'Yes.'

'Well, I'm going to give you this . . . '

He pointed to the box.

'They're keepsakes of Freddie . . . Little things I was able to put aside when they came along to sequestrate the old place . . . '

He was really moved. I even think there were tears in his eyes.

63

'I was very fond of him . . . I knew him as a youngster . . . He was a dreamer. He always told me he'd buy a sailing boat . . . He used to say: "Bob, you'll be my first mate . . . " God knows where he is now . . . if he's still alive . . . '

'We'll find him,' I said.

'He was too spoilt by his grandmother, you see . . . '

He took the box and handed it to me. I thought of Styoppa de Dzhagorev and the red box he too had given me. It certainly seemed everything ended with old chocolate or biscuit or cigar boxes.

'Thank you.'

'I'll walk you to the station.'

We took a forest path and he shone the beam of his torch ahead of us. Was he losing his way? It felt to me as though we were penetrating deeper and deeper into the forest.

'I'm trying to remember the name of Freddie's friend. The one you pointed out in the photograph . . . the South American . . . '

We were crossing a clearing, the foliage phosphorescent in the moonlight. A clump of stone-pines. He had switched off his torch, because it was almost as bright as daylight here.

'This is where Freddie used to come riding with another friend of his . . . A jockey . . . He never spoke to you about the jockey?'

'No.'

'I can't remember his name any more . . . And yet he was well known . . . He'd been Freddie's grandfather's jockey, when the old man had a racing stable . . . '

'Did the South American know the jockey too?'

'Of course. They used to come here together. The jockey played billiards with the other . . . I even think it was he who introduced the Russian woman to Freddie . . . '

I was afraid I would not remember all these details. I should have been noting them down on the spot.

64

The path sloped gently upwards and it was not easy walking, because of all the dead leaves underfoot.

'So, do you remember the South American's name?'

'Just a moment . . . it's coming back . . . '

I hugged the biscuit box to my hip, anxious to find out what its contents were. Perhaps I would discover some answers to my questions. My name. Or the jockey's name, for instance.

We were at the edge of a slope, at the bottom of which lay the station square. The station, with its bright neon-lit entrance hall, seemed deserted. A cyclist crossed the square slowly and stopped in front of the station.

'One moment . . . his first name was . . . Pedro . . . '

We stood at the edge of the slope. He had taken out his pipe again, and was cleaning it with a strange little instrument. Inwardly I repeated this name I'd been given at birth, this name by which I had been called throughout a whole section of my life and which, for a number of people, had conjured up my face. Pedro.

12

Not much here, in the biscuit box. A flaking, lead soldier with a drum. A four-leaved clover adhering to the centre of a white envelope. Some photographs.

I appear in two of them. No question that it is the same man as the one standing beside Gay Orlov and old Giorgiadze. A tall, dark-haired man, me, the only difference being that I've no moustache there. In one of the photographs, I am with another man as young as myself, as tall, but fair-haired. Freddie? Yes, as someone has written in pencil on the back of the photo: 'Pedro – Freddie – La Baule.' We are at the seaside and 'both wearing beach robes. Evidently a very old photograph.

In the second photograph, there are four of us: Freddie, myself, Gay Orlov, whom I recognized at once, and another young woman, all sitting on the floor, leaning against the red velvet sofa in the summer dining-room. To the right, you can make out a billiard-table.

A third photograph shows the young woman who is with us in the summer dining-room. She is standing in front of the billiard-table, holding a cue in her two hands. Fair hair falling to below the shoulders. The one I used to bring along to Freddie's château? In another photograph, she is leaning her elbows on the railings of a veranda.

A postcard addressed to 'Mr Robert Brun, c/o Howard de Luz, Valbreuse, Orne', showing the port of New York. It reads:

'My dear Bob. Regards from America. See you soon. Freddie.'

An odd document under the heading of:

Consulado general
de la
Republica Argentina
No. 106
The Consulate of the Republic of Argentina in France, in charge of Hellenic interests in the occupied zone, certifies that the archives of the Municipality of Salonica were destroyed by fire during the 1914–18 War.
Paris, 15 July, 1941.
Consulate of
the Republic of Argentina
in charge of Hellenic Interests.

A signature, and under it:

R. L. de Oliveira Cezar
Consul.

Me? No. His name is not Pedro.
A small newspaper cutting:

HOWARD DE LUZ SEQUESTRATION:
At Valbreuse (Orne) Château Saint-Lazare
7 and 11th April,
At the suit of
The Estate Management
Sale by public auction
of an important collection of
Objets d'art and furniture
antique and modern
Pictures – Porcelain – Ceramics
Carpets – Bedding – Household linen
Érard Grand Piano
Frigidaire etc.
Viewing: Saturday, 6th April, 14.00–18.00.
and 10.00–12.00 on the days of sale.

I open the envelope with the four-leaved clover. It contains four passport-size photographs: Freddie, myself, Gay Orlov, and the fair-haired young woman.

I also find an uncompleted passport of the Dominican Republic.

Casually turning over the photograph of the fair-haired young woman I discover the following, written in blue ink, in the same untidy handwriting as on the postcard from America:

PEDRO: ANJou 15-28.

13

How many engagement books still contain this telephone number which used to be mine? Was it simply the number of an office where I was to be found only one afternoon?

I dial ANJou 15-28. It rings and rings but no one answers. Are there any traces left of me in the deserted apartment, the room uninhabited for a long time, where this evening the telephone rings in vain?

I do not even need to call information. All I have to do is flex my calf muscle and spin Hutte's leather chair. In front of me, the rows of directories and year-books. One of them, smaller than the others, bound in pale-green goatskin. This is the one I need. All the telephone numbers in Paris for the last thirty years are itemized here, with the corresponding addresses.

I turn the pages, my heart thumping. And I read:

ANJou 15-28 – 10A, Rue Cambacérès, 8th arr.

But the street directory for the year does not list this telephone number:

CAMBACÉRÈS (Rue)
8th.

10A Association of Diamond Merchants	MIR 18-16
Couture-Fashion	ANJ 32-49
Pilgram (Hélène)	ELY 05-31
Rebbinder (Établis.)	MIR 12-08
Refuge (de)	ANJ 50-52
S.E.F.I.C.	MIR 74-31
	MIR 74-32
	MIR 74-33

14

A man whose Chistian name was Pedro. ANJou 15-28. 10A, Rue Cambacérès, eighth arrondissement.

It seems he worked for a South American legation. The clock Hutte had left on the desk points to two in the morning. Down below, in the Avenue Niel, only an occasional car passes and I can hear wheels squealing from time to time at the red lights.

I leaf through the old directories in the front of which are lists of embassies and legations, with their numbers.

Dominican Republic
Avenue de Messine, 21 (VIIIth). CARnot 10-18.
N . . . Special Envoy and Plenipotentiary.
Dr Gustavo J. Henriques. First Secretary.
Dr Salvador E. Paradas. Second Secretary.
(and Mme), Rue d'Alsace, 41 (Xth).
Dr Bienvenido Carrasco. Attaché.
R. Decamps, 45 (XVIth), tel. TRO 42-91.

Venezuela
Rue Copernic, 11 (XVIth). PASsy 72-29.
Chancellery: Rue de la Pompe, 115 (XVIth). PASsy 10-89.
Dr Carlo Aristimuno Coll, Special Envoy and Pleni-potentiary.
Mr Jaime Picon Febres. Counsellor.
Mr Antonio Maturib. First Secretary.
Mr Antonio Briuno. Attaché.
Colonel H. Lopez-Mendez. Military Attaché.
Mr Pedro Saloaga. Commercial Attaché.

Guatemala
Place Joffre, 12 (VIIth). Tel. SÉGur 09-59.
Mr Adam Maurisque Rios. Chargé d'Affaires.
Mr Ismael Gonzalez Arevalo. Secretary.
Mr Frederico Murgo. Attaché.

Ecuador
Avenue Wagram, 91 (XVIIth). Tel. ÉTOile 17-89.
Mr Gonzalo Zaldumbide. Special Envoy and Pleni-potentiary (and Mme).
Mr Alberto Puig Arosemena. First Secretary (and Mme).

Mr Alfredo Gangotena. Third Secretary (and Mme).
Mr Carlos Guzman. Attaché (and Mme).
Mr Victor Zevallos. Counsellor (and Mme), Avenue
d'Iéna, 21 (XVth).

El Salvador
Riquez Vega. Special Envoy.
Major J. H. Wishaw. Military Attaché (and daughter).
F. Capurro. First Secretary.
Luis . . .

The letters dance before my eyes. Who am I?

15

You turn left and it is amazing how silent and deserted
is this section of the Rue Cambacérès. Not a single car. I
walked past a hotel and my eyes were dazzled by a
chandelier, all its crystals blazing, in the lobby. It was
sunny.

10A is a narow, four-storey building. Tall windows
on the first floor. A policeman stands on sentry duty on
the pavement opposite.

One half of the double door to the building was open,
the hall light on. A long vestibule with grey walls. At
the end, a door with small glass panels which I found
hard to open. A carpetless stairway leading to the upper
floors.

I stopped in front of the first floor door. I had decided
to ask the tenants on each floor if ANJou 15-28 had been
their telephone number at any time, and there was a
tightness in my throat, as I was aware of the oddness of
this request. On the door, a brass plate, which read:
HÉLÈNE PILGRAM.

A high-pitched bell which was so worn, it rang only

intermittently. I pressed on it as long as possible. The
door opened a crack. A woman's face, her ash-grey hair
cut short, appeared in the opening.

'Excuse me . . . I wonder if you could tell me . . .'

Her very clear eyes fastened on me. Impossible to say
what her age was. Thirty, fifty?

'Was your old phone number ANJou 15-28, by any
chance?'

She frowned.

'Yes. Why?'

She opened the door. She was wearing a black, silk,
man's dressing-gown.

'Why do you want to know?'

'Because . . . I lived here once . . . '

She had moved out on to the landing and was staring
at me fixedly. Her eyes widened.

'But . . . you're . . . Mr . . . McEvoy?'

'Yes,' I said on the off-chance.

'Come in.'

She seemed quite overcome. We stood, the two of us,
facing each other, in the middle of a lobby with spoilt
parquet flooring. Some of the pieces had been replaced
by strips of linoleum.

'You haven't changed much,' she said, smiling.

'Nor have you.'

'Do you still remember me?'

'I remember you very well,' I said.

'That's nice . . . '

Her eyes lingered affectionately on me.

'Come . . . '

She preceded me into a very large, very high-ceilinged
room, whose windows were the ones I had noticed from
the street. The parquet, as spoilt as in the hall, was
hidden here and there under white woollen rugs.
Through the windows, the autumn sun lit the room
with an amber light.

'Do sit down . . . '

She pointed to a long wall-sofa with velvet cushions.

She sat down on my left.

'It's funny to see you again so . . . unexpectedly . . . '

'I happened to be in the district,' I said.

She looked younger to me than she had seemed in the doorway. Not a line at the junctions of the lips, around the eyes, or on the brow, and this smooth face contrasted with her white hair.

'It seems to me you've changed your hair colour,' I hazarded.

'No, I haven't . . . My hair's been white since I was twenty-five . . . I preferred to keep it that colour . . . '

Apart from the velvet sofa, there was not much furniture. A rectangular table against the opposite wall. An old dress-stand between the two windows, the torso covered with a piece of dirty beige material. The unusual presence of this object made one think of a dressmaker's. Besides, I noticed, in a corner of the room, a sewing machine on a table.

'Do you remember the apartment?' she asked. 'You see . . . I've kept some of the things . . . '

She motioned towards the dress-stand.

'Denise left all that . . . '

Denise?

'No, it hasn't really changed much . . . ' I said.

'And Denise?' she asked impatiently. 'What happened to her?'

'Well,' I said, 'I haven't seen her for a long while . . . '

'Oh . . . '

She looked disappointed and shook her head as though realizing she should not say anything further about this 'Denise'.

'Actually,' I said, 'you knew Denise a long time, didn't you? . . . '

'Yes . . . I knew her through Léon . . . '

'Léon?'

'Léon Van Allen.'

'Of course,' I said, responding to her tone of voice which was almost reproachful when the name 'Léon' had not instantly evoked 'Léon Van Allen' for me.

'What's he doing, Léon Van Allen?' I asked.

'Oh . . . I've not had any news of him for two or three years . . . He'd gone to Dutch Guyana, Paramaribo . . . He started a dancing school there . . . '

'Dancing?'

'Yes. Before he was a couturier, Léon danced . . . Didn't you know that?'

'Yes, I did. But I had forgotten.'

She threw herself back, leaning against the wall, and re-tied the belt of her dressing-gown.

'And what about you? What have you been doing?'

'Oh, me? . . . Nothing . . . '

'You no longer work at the Dominican Embassy?'

'No.'

'Do you remember when you offered to get me a Dominican passport? . . . You used to say that one had to be ready in life and always have several passports, as a precaution . . . '

This memory amused her. She gave a short laugh.

'When did you last have any news of . . . Denise?' I asked her.

'You'd left for Megève with her and she dropped me a line from there. Since then, nothing.'

She stared at me questioningly, but no doubt did not dare ask me directly. Who was this Denise? Had she played an important part in my life?

'You see,' I said, 'there are times when I feel as though I'm in a complete fog . . . There are gaps in my memory . . . Periods of depression . . . So, since I was passing, I thought I'd come up . . . to try to find the . . . the . . . '

I was looking for the right word in vain, but it did not matter at all, since she smiled and this smile showed that my approach was no surprise to her.

'You mean: to try to find the good times again.'

'Yes. That's it . . . The good times . . . '

She picked up a gilt box on a small low table at the

end of the sofa and opened it. It was filled with cigarettes.

'No thanks,' I said.

'You don't smoke any more? They're English cigarettes. I remember you used to smoke English cigarettes . . . Whenever the three of us met here, you, me and Denise, you used to bring me a bagful of packets of English cigarettes . . . '

'Yes, that's right . . . '

'You could get as many as you wanted at the Dominican Legation . . . '

I stretched my hand out to the gilt box and picked up a cigarette between thumb and forefinger. I put it apprehensively in my mouth. She handed me her lighter after having lit her own cigarette. I had to try several times before I managed to get a flame. I inhaled. At once, a very painful, smarting sensation made me cough.

'I've lost the habit of it,' I said.

I did not know how to get rid of this cigarette and continued to hold it between thumb and forefinger while it burnt itself out.

'So,' I said, 'you live in this apartment now?'

'Yes. I moved in again when I had no more news of Denise . . . Anyway, she'd told me before she left, that I could take the apartment back . . . '

'Before she left?'

'Naturally . . . Before you left for Megève . . . '

She shrugged her shoulders, as though this must be obvious to me.

'I have the feeling I was only in this apartment a short time . . . '

'You stayed here several months with Denise . . . '

'And you lived here before us?'

She looked at me in amazement.

'Of course I did, you know that . . . It was my apartment . . . I lent it to Denise because I had to leave Paris . . . '

'Forgive me . . . My mind was on something else.'

'It suited Denise here . . . She had room for her dressmaking . . . '

A dressmaker?

'I wonder why we left this apartment,' I said.

'Me too . . . '

Again the questioning look. But what could I say in explanation? I knew less than she did. I knew nothing about all this. I finally put the fag-end of my cigarette, which was burning my fingers, in the ash tray.

'Did we meet before we came to live here?' I said tentatively.

'Yes. Two or three times. In your hotel . . . '

'What hotel.'

'Rue Cambon. The Hôtel Castille. Do you remember the green room you had with Denise?'

'Yes.'

'You'd left the Hôtel Castille because you didn't feel safe there . . . That was why, wasn't it?'

'Yes.'

'It really was a strange time . . . '

'What time?'

She did not answer and lit another cigarette.

'I'd like to show you some photos,' I said.

From the inside pocket of my jacket, I pulled out an envelope which I was never without now and in which I had put all the photos. I showed her the one of Freddie Howard de Luz, Gay Orlov, the unknown young woman and me, taken in the 'summer dining-room'.

'Do you recognize me?'

She had turned to look at the photo in the sunlight.

'You're with Denise but I don't know the two others . . . '

So, that was Denise.

'You didn't know Freddie Howard de Luz?'

'No.'

'Or Gay Orlov?'

'No.'

People certainly lead compartmentalized lives and their friends do not know each other. It's unfortunate.

'I've another two photos of her.'

I handed her the tiny passport photo and the other with her leaning her elbows on the railings.

'I've already seen that photo,' she said . . . 'I think she even sent it to me from Megève . . . But I don't remember what I did with it now . . . '

I took the photo from her and looked at it closely. Megève. Behind Denise was a small window with wooden shutters. Yes, the shutters and the railings might well belong to a mountain chalet.

'That journey to Megève really was an odd idea,' I announced suddenly. 'Did Denise ever tell you what she thought of it?'

She was studying the little passport photo. I waited for her to answer, my heart beating hard. She raised her head.

'Yes . . . She spoke to me about it . . . She told me that Megève was a safe place . . . And that you could always cross the frontier . . . '

'Yes . . . Of course . . . '

I did not dare continue. Why am I so diffident and apprehensive, when it comes to something that means a lot to me? She too – I could tell from her look – would have welcomed some explanation. The two of us remained silent. Finally, she took the plunge:

'But what did happen at Megève?'

She put this question so urgently that for the first time I felt discouraged, and even more than that, desperate, the kind of despair that overwhelms you when you realize that in spite of your efforts, your good qualities, all your goodwill, you are running into an insurmountable obstacle.

'I'll tell you about it . . . Another day . . . '

There must have been something distraught in my voice or my expression, because she squeezed my arm as though to console me and said:

'Forgive me asking you indiscreet questions . . . But
. . . I was a friend of Denise . . . '
'I understand . . . '
She had got up.
'Wait a moment . . . '
She left the room. I looked down at the patches of
sunlight on the white wool rugs. Then at the parquet
and the rectangular table, and the old dress-stand which
had belonged to 'Denise'. Surely, I must finally recog-
nize one of the places where I had lived.
She returned, holding something in her hand. Two
books. And a diary.
'Denise forgot this when she left. Here . . . you have
them . . . '
I was surprised she had not put these souvenirs in a
box, as Styoppa de Dzhagorev and the former gardener
of Freddie's mother had done. Indeed, it was the first
time in the course of my investigations that I had not
been given a box. This thought made me laugh.
'What are you laughing at?'
'Nothing.'
I studied the covers of the books. One showed the
face of a Chinaman, with a moustache and bowler hat,
looming out of a blueish fog. The title: *Charlie Chan*.
The other cover was yellow and at the bottom was a
design of a mask and a goose quill. The book was called,
Anonymous Letters.
'Denise simply consumed detective novels . . . ,' she
said. 'There's this too . . . '
She handed me the little crocodile-skin diary.
'Thanks.'
I opened it and turned over the pages. Nothing had
been written there: no name, no appointments. The
diary showed the days and the months, but not the year.
Finally I discovered a piece of paper between the pages
and unfolded it:

Republic of France

Seine Department. Prefecture.

Abstract of the records of births in the XIIIth arrondissement of Paris

Year 1917

21st December nineteen hundred and seventeen

At fifteen hours, Quai d'Austerlitz 9A, was born

Denise Yvette Coudreuse, of female sex, to

Paul Coudreuse, and to Henriette Bofaerts, no profession, domicile as above

Married 3rd April 1939 in Paris (XVIIth), to Jimmy
Pedro Stern.

Certified true abstract

Paris – the sixteenth of June 1939

'Did you see this?' I said.

She looked at the certificate in surprise.

'Did you know her husband? This . . . Jimmy Pedro
Stern?'

'No.'

I put the diary and the certificate into my inside
pocket, with the envelope which contained the photographs, and for some reason the thought struck me that,
as soon as I could, I should conceal all these treasures in
the lining of my jacket.

'Thanks for giving me these souvenirs.'

'You're welcome, Mr McEvoy.'

I was relieved when she repeated my name, as I had
not quite caught it when she first mentioned it. I should
have liked to write it down, there and then, but was
unsure about the spelling.

'I like the way you pronounce my name,' I said. 'It's
hard for a French person . . . But how would you write
it? People always spell it wrong when they try . . . '

A mischievous tone had crept into my voice. She
smiled.

'M . . . C . . . capital E, V . . . O . . . Y . . . ' she
spelt.

'In one word? Are you quite sure?'

'Absolutely,' she said, as though sidestepping a trap I had set for her.

So, it was McEvoy.

'Well done,' I said.

'I never make spelling mistakes.'

'Pedro McEvoy . . . It's a strange name, all the same, don't you think? There are times when I still can't get used to it . . . '

'By the way, I was forgetting this,' she said.

She took an envelope from her pocket.

'It's the last little note I had from Denise . . . '

I unfolded the sheet of paper and read:

Megève, 14th February.

Dear Hélène,

It's decided. Tomorrow Pedro and I are crossing the frontier. I'll send you news from over there, as soon as possible.

In the meantime, I'll give you the telephone number of someone in Paris through whom we can correspond:

OLEG DE WRÉDÉ   AUTeuil 54-73

Affectionately,

Denise

'And did you phone?'

'Yes, but each time I was told the gentleman wasn't there.'

'Who was he this . . . Wrédé?'

'I don't know. Denise never spoke to me about him . . . '

The sun had gradually deserted the room. She lit the little lamp standing on the low table at the end of the sofa.

'I should very much like to see the room where I lived,' I said.

'Of course . . . '

We walked down a corridor and she opened a door on the right.

'There,' she said. 'I no longer use this room . . . I sleep in the guest room . . . You know . . . the one which looks out on the yard . . . '

I stood in the doorway. It was still quite light. Purplish red curtains hung on both sides of the window. The wallpaper had a pale blue design.

'Do you remember it?' she asked.

'Yes.'

A divan-bed against the back wall. I sat down on the edge of this bed.

'Can I sit here for a few minutes on my own?'

'Of course.'

'It reminds me of "the good times" . . . '

She gave me a sad look and shook her head.

'I'll make some tea . . . '

She left the room and I looked around me. In this room too, the parquet floor was damaged and there were pieces missing, though the gaps had not been filled. Across from the window, a marble fireplace with a mirror above it, whose gilt frame was embellished with a shell in each corner. I lay down on the bed and stared up at the ceiling, then at the wallpaper design. I studied the latter so closely, my forehead practically touched the wall. Rustic scenes. Girls in elaborate wigs, seated on swings. Shepherds in puffed knee-breeches, playing the mandoline. Moonlit woods. None of this reminded me of anything and yet these designs must have been familiar to me when I used to sleep in this bed. I searched the ceiling, the walls, and the door area for any sign, any trace, though of what I did not know. But nothing caught my eye.

I got up and walked to the window. I looked out.

The street was deserted and darker than when I had entered the building. The policeman was still standing sentry on the opposite pavement. To the left, if I leant out, I could see a square, also deserted, with other policemen on sentry-go. The windows of all these buildings seemed to be absorbing the gathering dusk.

They were dark and it was clear that nobody lived around here.

Then it was as if something clicked into place. The view from this room made me feel anxious, apprehensive, a feeling I had had before. These façades, this deserted street, these figures standing sentry in the dusk disturbed me in the same insidious manner as a song or a once familiar perfume. And I was certain that I had often stood here, at this hour, motionless, watching, without making the slightest movement, and without even daring to switch on the light.

When I returned to the drawing-room, I thought no one was there any longer, but she was stretched out on the velvet sofa. She was asleep. I approached quietly, and sat down at the other end of the sofa. A tray with a tea-pot and two cups, in the centre of the white woollen carpet. I coughed. She did not wake up. Then I poured tea into the two cups. It was cold.

The lamp beside the sofa left a whole section of the room in darkness and I could just make out the table, the dress-stand and the sewing machine, the objects which 'Denise' had abandoned here. What had our evenings in this room been like? How could I find out?

I sipped the tea. I could hear her breath, almost imperceptible, but the room was so silent that the slightest sound, the slightest whisper would have stood out with disturbing clarity. What was the good of waking her? She could not tell me much. I put my cup down on the woollen carpet.

The parquet creaked under me just as I was leaving the room and stepping into the corridor.

Groping, I looked for the door, then the time-switch on the stairway. I shut the door as quietly as possible. Hardly had I opened the other door, the glass-panelled one, to cross the entrance-hall, than something again clicked into place, as it had done when I looked out of the window of the room. The entrance-hall was lit by a globe in the ceiling which shed a white light. Gradually, my eyes got used to this over-bright light. I stood there, gazing at the grey walls and the shining panels of the door.

A mental picture flashed before me, like those fragments of some fleeting dream which one tries to hold on to in waking, so as to be able to reconstruct the whole dream. I saw myself, walking through a dark Paris, and opening the door to this building in the Rue Cambacérès. Then my eyes were suddenly blinded and for a few seconds I could see nothing, so great was the contrast between this white light and the night outside.

What period did this go back to? To the time when my name was Pedro McEvoy and I came back here every evening? Did I recognize the entrance, the big rectangular door-mat, the grey walls, the globe-lamp in the ceiling, with a brass ring around it? Behind the glass panels of the door, I could see the staircase and I wanted to climb it slowly, to go through all the motions I used to and retrace my steps.

I believe that the entrance-halls of buildings still retain the echo of footsteps of those who used to cross them and who have since vanished. Something continues to vibrate after they have gone, fading waves, but which can still be picked up if one listens carefully. Perhaps, after all, I never was this Pedro McEvoy, I was nothing, but waves passed through me, sometimes faint, sometimes stronger, and all these scattered echoes afloat in the air crystallized and there I was.

16

Hôtel Castille, Rue Cambon. Across from the reception desk, a morning-room. In the glass-fronted bookcase,

L. de Viel-Castel's *History of the Restoration*. Perhaps, one evening, I had taken down one of these volumes before going up to my room, and had forgotten the letter, photograph, or telegram I had used to mark my place in it. But I haven't the audacity to ask the house-porter if I can leaf through the seventeen volumes.

At the back of the hotel, a courtyard surrounded by a wall with green, ivy-covered trellises. Ochre paving-stones underfoot, the colour of tennis court gravel. Tables and garden chairs.

So, I had lived here with this Denise Coudreuse. Did our room look out on to the Rue Cambon or the courtyard?

17

9A, Quai d'Austerlitz. A three-storeyed building with the main entrance opening on to a yellow-walled passageway. A café whose sign reads *A la Marine*. Behind the glass door hangs a notice in bright red letters: 'MEN SPREEKT VLAAMCH.'

A dozen or so people crowded around the bar. I sat down at one of the empty tables, against the back wall, on which was a large photograph of a port: ANTWERP, as it said under the photo.

The customers at the bar were talking in very loud voices. They all worked locally, no doubt, and were having their pre-dinner drink. By the glass door, a slot machine with a man in a navy-blue suit and tie standing at it, his clothing contrasting with the lumber-jackets, leather jackets or overalls worn by the others. He was playing calmly, pulling the spring rod back with an easy movement.

The cigarette and pipe smoke irritated my eyes and made me cough a little. There was a smell of lard in the air.

'What would you like?'

I had not seen him coming up. I had even thought that no one would come to ask me what I wanted, so little notice had been taken of my presence at a table in the rear.

'An espresso,' I said.

He was a short man, of about sixty, with white hair, his red face already flushed by the various aperitifs he had no doubt imbibed. His light blue eyes seemed even paler against the ruddiness of his complexion. There was something jolly in these crockery tints – white, red and blue.

'Excuse me . . . ,' I said, just as he was about to return to the bar. 'What does the notice on the door mean?'

'MEN SPREEKT VLAAMCH?'

He had pronounced these words in a resounding voice.

'Yes.'

'It means: Flemish spoken.'

At that, he left me and made for the bar with a rolling gait. Without any fuss he eased aside the customers in his path.

He returned with the cup of coffee, which he held in both hands, his arms stretched out in front of him, as though he was trying not to drop the cup.

'Here you are.'

He placed the cup in the centre of the table, breathing as hard as a marathon runner at the end of the race.

'Does the name . . . COUDREUSE . . . mean anything to you?'

I had put the question bluntly.

He sank into the chair opposite me and folded his arms. He was still breathing hard.

'Why? You knew . . . Coudreuse?'

'No, but I've heard about him in the family.'

His colour was brick-red now and sweat was standing out on the wings of his nose.

'Coudreuse . . . He used to live up there, on the second floor . . . '

He had a slight accent. I swallowed a mouthful of coffee, determined to let him talk, since another question might put him off.

'He worked at the Gare d'Austerlitz . . . His wife was from Antwerp, like me . . . '

'He had a daughter, didn't he?'

He smiled.

'Yes. A pretty little thing . . . Did you know her?'

'No, but I heard about her . . . '

'What's happened to her?'

'That's what I'm trying to find out.'

'She used to come here every morning for her father's cigarettes. Coudreuse smoked Laurens's, Belgian cigarettes . . . '

He was caught up in his memories and, like me, I think, no longer heard the bursts of talk and laughter nor the machine-gun rattle of the slot machine close by.

'A decent fellow, Coudreuse . . . I often ate with them, upstairs . . . His wife, she spoke Flemish . . . '

'You've no news of them since then?'

'He died . . . His wife returned to Antwerp . . . '

And he made a broad, sweeping gesture across the table.

'It's the dim and distant past, all that . . . '

'You say she used to come for her father's cigarettes . . . What was the make again?'

'Laurens's.'

I hoped I'd remember the name.

'A funny kid . . . at ten, she was already playing billiards with my customers . . . '

He pointed to a door at the back of the café which must have led to the billiards room. So, that was where she had learnt the game.

'Wait a moment,' he said. 'I'll show you something . . . '

He rose heavily and walked over to the bar. Again he eased aside all those who were in his way. Most of the customers were wearing sailors' caps and speaking some strange language, Flemish no doubt. I thought that it was because of the barges anchored below, by the Quai d'Austerlitz, which must have come from Belgium.

'Here . . . Look . . . '

He had sat down opposite and handed me an old fashion-magazine, the cover of which showed a girl, with chestnut-brown hair and limpid eyes, and with something Asiatic in her features. I recognized her at once: Denise. She was wearing a black bolero and holding an orchid.

'That was Denise, Coudreuse's daughter . . . See . . . A pretty little thing . . . She became a model . . . I knew her when she was just a kid . . . '

The magazine cover was spotted and streaked with whisky.

'I still remember her as she was when she used to come for the Laurens's . . . '

'She wasn't a dressmaker, was she?'

'No, I don't think so.'

'And you really don't know what became of her?'

'No.'

'You haven't got her mother's address, in Antwerp?'

He shook his head. He looked broken-hearted.

'It's all over and done with, my friend . . . '

What did he mean?

'Would you lend me this magazine?' I asked him.

'Yes, pal, but you must promise to return it.'

'It's a promise.'

'I'm attached to it. It's like a family souvenir.'

'What time did she come for the cigarettes?'

'Always at quarter-to-eight. Before going to school.'

'Which school?'

'Rue Jenner. Sometimes her father took her.'

86

I stretched out my hand for the magazine and snatched it up quickly, my heart beating hard. He might, after all, change his mind and decide to keep it.

'Thanks. I'll bring it back tomorrow.'

'Mind you do, huh?'

He looked at me suspiciously.

'But why are you interested? Are you family?'

'Yes.'

I could not resist studying the magazine cover. Denise seemed a little younger than in the photograph I already had. She was wearing ear-rings, her neck half hidden by fern leaves which rose above the orchid she was carrying. In the background, there was a carved wooden angel. And at the bottom, in the left-hand corner of the photograph, in tiny red lettering which stood out well against the black of her bolero, were the words: 'Photo by Jean-Michel Mansoure.'

'Would you like something to drink?' he asked.

'No thanks.'

'Well, the coffee's on the house.'

'That's very kind of you.'

I rose, holding the magazine. He walked ahead of me, opening up a path for me through his customers, who were growing thicker and thicker around the bar. He spoke to them in Flemish. It took us a while to reach the glass door. He opened it and mopped his nose.

'You won't forget to give it back, will you?' he said, pointing to the magazine.

He closed the glass door and followed me out into the street.

'You see. They lived up there . . . on the second floor . . . '

The windows were lit up. At the back of one of the rooms, I could make out a wardrobe of dark wood.

'There are other tenants . . . '

'When you used to eat with them, what room was it?'

'That one . . . on the left . . . '

And he pointed to the window.

'And Denise's room?'

'It looked out on the other side . . . On the court-yard . . . '

He looked thoughtful, standing there next to me. Finally I held out my hand.

'Good-bye. I'll return the magazine.'

'Good-bye.'

He went back into the café. He looked at me, his big red head pressed against the door. The smoke from the pipes and cigarettes submerged the customers at the bar in a yellow fog and this big red head, in its turn, grew more and more hazy, because of the blur his breath left on the glass.

It was night. The time Denise returned from school, if she stayed for night classes. What route did she take? Did she come from the right or the left? I had forgotten to ask the café owner. At that time, there was less traffic and the leaves of the plane-trees formed an arch over the Quai d'Austerlitz. The station itself, further off, must have looked like the station of some town in the South-West. Beyond that, the Botanical Gardens and the darkness and profound silence of the Wine Market added to the peacefulness of the neighbourhood.

I entered the building and flicked on the time-switch. A corridor with old black and grey tiles. A door-mat, made of iron. Letter boxes on the yellow wall. And the everlasting smell of lard.

If I closed my eyes, I thought, if I concentrated, placing my fingers against my forehead, perhaps I would manage to hear, far off, the slap of sandals on the stairs.

18

But I think it was in a hotel bar that Denise and I met for the first time. I was with the man who appears in the photographs, my childhood friend, Freddie Howard de Luz, and Gay Orlov. They had been living for some time in the hotel, as they had come back from America. Gay Orlov told me she was waiting for a friend, a girl she had just got to know.

She walked towards us and her face struck me at once. An Asiatic face, although she was almost blonde. Almond eyes, very clear. High cheekbones. She wore a strange little hat, shaped somewhat like a Tyrolean one, and her hair was cut rather short.

Freddie and Gay Orlov told us to wait for them a moment and went up to their room. The two of us were left, facing one another. She smiled.

We did not speak. She had clear eyes, with a greenness that came and went in them.

19

Mr Jean-Michel. 1, Rue Gabrielle, XVIII. CLI 72-01.

20

'You must forgive me,' he said when I sat down at his table in a café in the Place Blanche where he had suggested, over the telephone, that I join him at around 6 o'clock. 'You must forgive me, but I always arrange to meet people out . . . Particularly the first time . . . Now we can go to my place . . . '

I had recognized him easily, as he had indicated that he would be wearing a dark green velvet suit and that

89

his hair was white, very white, and cut short. This severe cut contrasted strongly with his long black eyelashes, which fluttered ceaselessly, his almond eyes and the feminine shape of his mouth: upper lip sinuous, lower tense and imperious.

Standing, he seemed to be of medium height. He put on a raincoat and we left the café.

When we were standing in the Boulevard de Clichy, he pointed to a building, near the Moulin Rouge, and said:

'In the old days, I'd have arranged to meet you at Graff's . . . Over there . . . But it no longer exists . . . '

We crossed the street and took the Rue Coustou. He quickened his pace, glancing furtively over at the sea-green bars on the left-hand side of the road, and by the time we were level with the big garage, he was almost running . . . He did not stop until we had reached the corner of the Rue Lepic.

'Forgive me,' he said, out of breath, 'but this street has some odd memories for me . . . Forgive me . . . '

He had really been frightened. I believe he was even trembling.

'It gets better from now on . . . I'm all right now . . . '

He smiled, looking at the Rue Lepic rising before him with its market stalls and the well-lit food stores.

We set off along the Rue des Abbesses. He walked in a calm and relaxed manner. I wanted to ask him what 'odd memories' the Rue Coustou had for him but I did not wish to be indiscreet or reduce him once again to that nervous state which had so surprised me. And suddenly, before we had reached the Place des Abbesses, he picked up speed again. I was walking on his right. As we were crossing the Rue Germain-Pilon, I saw him cast a horrified look at that narrow street with its low, dark houses, which descends rather steeply to the boulevard below. He held my arm very tightly. He clung to me, as though in an effort to tear his gaze away from this street. I drew him across to the other pavement.

'Thank you . . . You know . . . it's very funny . . . '

He hesitated, on the edge of confiding something.

'I . . . I feel dizzy every time I cross this end of the Rue Germain-Pilon . . . I . . . I have the urge to walk down it . . . It's stronger than I am . . . '

'Why don't you walk down it?'

'Because . . . the Rue Germain-Pilon . . . Because once there was . . . There was a place . . . '

He broke off.

'Oh . . . ,' he said with an evasive smile. 'It's idiotic of me . . . Montmartre has changed such a lot . . . It would take ages to explain . . . You didn't know the old Montmartre . . . '

How could he be so certain?

He lived in the Rue Gabrielle, in a building over-looking the gardens of the Sacré Cœur. We used the back stairway. It took him a long time to open the door: three locks and a different key for each one, which he turned deliberately and with the concentration needed to open a complicated safe.

A tiny apartment. It consisted only of a drawing-room and bedroom, which must originally have been one room. Pink satin curtains, held back by cords of silver thread, separated the two rooms. The drawing-room walls were covered in sky-blue silk and the only window was hidden by curtains of the same colour. Black lacquer pedestal-tables on which stood ivory or jade objects, tub easy-chairs upholstered in pale green, and a settee covered with a floral design material of a still paler green, gave the whole room the appearance of a sweetshop. The light came from gilt bracket-lamps on the wall.

'Sit down,' he said.

I sat down on the floral-design settee. He sat beside me.

'So . . . let me see it . . . '

I extracted the fashion magazine from my pocket and showed him the cover, on which Denise appeared. He

91

took the magazine from me and put on glasses with heavy tortoise-shell frames.

'Yes . . . yes . . . Photo by Jean-Michel Mansoure . . . That's me, all right . . . There's no doubt about it at all . . . '

'Do you remember the girl?'

'I don't. I rarely worked for this magazine . . . It was a small fashion journal . . . I worked mainly for *Vogue*, you understand . . . '

He wanted to make the distinction clear.

'And you can't tell me anything else about this photo?'

He looked at me with an amused expression. In the light from the bracket-lamps, I could see that the skin of his face was covered with tiny lines and freckles.

'My dear chap, I can tell you straight away . . . '

He rose, the magazine in his hand, turned the key in a door which I had not noticed until then, because it was covered with sky-blue silk, like the walls. It led into a small room. I heard him pulling out numerous metal drawers. After a few minutes, he emerged from the room, closing the door carefully behind him.

'Here,' he said. 'I've the voucher slip with the negatives. I've kept everything, from the beginning . . . It's arranged by year and in alphabetical order . . . '

He sat down beside me again and studied the slip.

'Denise . . . Coudreuse . . . That's the one, isn't it?'

'Yes.'

'She never had any other photo sessions with me . . . Now I remember the girl . . . She did a lot of photos with Hoynigen-Hunne . . . '

'Who?'

'Hoynigen-Hunne, a German photographer . . . Yes, of course . . . That's it . . . She did a lot of work with Hoynigen-Hunne . . . '

Each time Mansoure pronounced this word with its plaintive, lunar resonance, I felt Denise's clear eyes on me, like that first time.

'I've the address she gave me then, if it's of any interest . . . '

'It is,' I answered in an eager voice.

'97, Rue de Rome, Paris, XVIIth arrondissement. 97, Rue de Rome . . . '

Suddenly he raised his head and looked at me. His face was frighteningly white, his eyes wide open.

'97, Rue de Rome . . . '

'What's the matter? . . . ' I asked.

'Now I remember the girl very well . . . I had a friend who lived in the same building . . . '

He looked at me in a suspicious manner and seemed as agitated as when he had crossed the Rue Coustou and the top of the Rue Germain-Pilon.

'An odd coincidence . . . I remember it very well . . . I picked her up at her place, in the Rue de Rome, to take the photos and I took the opportunity of dropping in on this friend . . . He lived on the floor above.'

'You went to her place?'

'Yes. But we took the photos in my friend's apartment . . . He stayed with us . . . '

'Who was the friend?'

He was growing paler and paler. He was frightened.

'I'll . . . explain . . . But first I must have a drink . . . to steady myself . . . '

He rose and walked across to a little table on casters, which he wheeled over in front of the settee. On the upper tray were some small carafes with crystal stoppers and silver labels engraved with the names of the liqueurs, like the chains the Wehrmacht musicians used to wear round their necks.

'I've only got sweet liqueurs . . . Do you mind?'

'Not at all.'

'I'm going to have a little Marie Brizard . . . how about you?'

'I'll have the same.'

He poured the Marie Brizard into narrow glasses and when I sipped this liqueur, it blended in with the

93

somewhat nauseating satins, ivories and gilt around me. It expressed the very essence of this apartment.

'This friend of mine who lived in the Rue de Rome . . . was murdered . . . '

He had uttered the last word hesitantly and was clearly making an effort on my account, or he would not have had the courage to use so unambiguous a word.

'He was a Greek from Egypt . . . He wrote poetry, and a couple of books . . . '

'And do you think Denise Coudreuse knew him?'

'Oh . . . She must have run into him on the stairs,' he said impatiently, since this detail was of no significance to him.

'And . . . Did it happen in the building?'

'Yes.'

'Was Denise Coudreuse living in the building at the time?'

He had not even heard my question.

'It happened at night . . . He had brought someone up to his apartment . . . He brought anyone up to his apartment . . . '

'Was the murderer found? . . . '

He shrugged.

'That kind of murderer is never found . . . I was sure this would happen to him in the end . . . If you'd seen what some of those boys he invited up there in the evening looked like . . . I'd have been scared even during the day . . . '

He gave a strange smile, wracked with emotion and at the same time full of horror.

'What was your friend's name?' I asked him.

'Alec Scouffi. A Greek from Alexandria.'

He got up suddenly and pulled aside the sky-blue silk curtains which covered the window . . . Then he returned to his place beside me on the settee.

'You must forgive me . . . But there are times when I get the feeling someone is hiding behind the curtains . . . A little more Marie Brizard? Yes, a drop more . . . '

94

He forced himself to sound jolly and gripped my arm as if to prove to himself that I was really there, beside him.

'Scouffi had set up in France . . . I knew him in Montmartre . . . He wrote a very nice book called *Ship at Anchor* . . . '

'But Mr Mansoure,' I said in a firm voice, articulating each syllable clearly, so that this time he would have to respond to my question, 'if, as you tell me, Denise Coudreuse lived on the floor below, she must have heard something unusual that night . . . She must have been questioned as a witness . . . '

'Perhaps she was.'

He shrugged his shoulders. No, it was clear that this Denise Coudreuse who meant so much to me and whose every movement I would have liked to have known, didn't interest him at all.

'The most awful thing about it is that I know the murderer . . . You wouldn't have believed it, because he'd the face of an angel . . . But when he looked at you with those hard, grey eyes . . . '

He shivered. It was as though the man he was talking about was there, in front of us, and was transfixing him with his grey eyes.

'A vile little rotter . . . The last time I saw him was during the Occupation, in a basement restaurant in the Rue Cambon . . . He was with a German . . . '

His voice trembled at the memory, and even though I was obsessed with thoughts of Denise Coudreuse, this shrill voice, this passionate protest, as it were, impressed me in a way I could hardly justify to myself, and which made it clear that he was, in fact, jealous of his friend's fate and resented the man with the grey eyes for not having murdered *him*.

'He's still alive . . . Still in Paris . . . I found out through someone . . . Of course, he no longer has that angel face . . . Would you like to hear his voice?'

I had no time to respond to his surprising question:

he had picked up the telephone, on a red leather pouf next to us, and was dialling a number. He handed me the receiver.

'You'll hear it . . . Listen . . . He calls himself "Blue Rider" . . . '

At first all I heard were the short bursts of ringing which indicated that the line was engaged. And then, in the intervals between the ringing, I began to make out the voices of men and women sending messages to each other: 'Maurice and Josy would like René to phone . . . '; 'Lucien is waiting for Jeannot at the Rue de la Convention . . . '; 'Mrs du Barry is looking for a partner . . . '; 'Alcibiades is alone this evening . . . '

Skeletal conversations, voices seeking each other out, in spite of the ringing which obliterated them at regular intervals. And all these faceless beings trying to exchange telephone numbers, passwords, in the hope of some rendezvous. Finally I heard a voice that was more distant than the others and which kept repeating:

'"Blue Rider" is free this evening . . . "Blue Rider" is free this evening . . . Give your phone number . . . Give your phone number . . . '

'Do you hear him?' asked Mansoure. 'Do you hear him?'

He pressed his ear to the receiver, bringing his face up to mine.

'The number I dialled hasn't belonged to anyone for a long time,' he explained. 'And they found out they could communicate that way.'

He stopped speaking, so as to be able to listen to 'Blue Rider' better. For me all these voices were voices from beyond the grave, voices of vanished people – wandering voices which could respond to each other only through a discontinued telephone number.

'It's dreadful, dreadful . . . ,' he repeated, pressing the phone to his ear. 'The murderer . . . Do you hear? . . . '

He hung up abruptly. He was bathed in sweat.

'I'll show you a photograph of the friend this little villain murdered . . . And I'll try to find his novel, *Ship at Anchor*, for you . . . You should read it . . . '

He rose and went into the other room which was separated from the drawing-room by the pink satin curtains. I noticed a very low bed with a guanaco fur thrown over it, half hidden by the curtains.

I had walked over to the window and was looking down at the rails of the Montmartre funicular, the gardens of the Sacré Cœur and, further off, the whole of Paris, with its lights, its roofs, its shadows. Denise Coudreuse and I had met one day in this maze of roads and boulevards. Paths that cross, among those of thousands and thousands of people all over Paris, like countless little balls on a gigantic, electric billiard-table, which occasionally bump into each other. And nothing remained of this, not even the luminous trail a firefly leaves behind it.

Mansoure, out of breath, re-emerged from behind the pink curtains, holding a book and several photographs.

'I've found them! . . . I've found them! . . . '

He was radiant. He had no doubt feared that he had mislaid these relics. He sat down opposite me and handed me the book.

'There you are . . . It's a prize possession, but I'll lend you it . . . You simply must read it . . . It's a fine book . . . And he really had a presentiment . . . Alec foresaw his own death . . . '

His face darkened.

'I'll give you two or three photos of him as well . . . '

'But don't you want to keep them?'

'No, no! Don't worry . . . I've dozens like them . . . And all the negatives! . . . '

I wanted to ask him to print a few photos of Denise Coudreuse for me, but did not have the nerve.

'It's a pleasure to give a fellow like you photos of Alec . . . '

'Thanks.'

'You were looking out of the window? A nice view, isn't it? And to think that Alec's murderer is somewhere out there . . . '

And with a movement of the back of his hand against the window, he took in the whole of Paris, below.

'He must be an old man, now . . . an awful old man . . . made up . . . '

With a shudder, he closed the pink satin curtains.

'I prefer not to think about it.'

'I'll have to be going back,' I said. 'Thanks again for the photos.'

'You're leaving me alone? You wouldn't like a last drop of Marie Brizard?'

'No thanks.'

He accompanied me to the service door, along a corridor hung in dark blue velvet and lit by bracket-lamps with garlands of little crystals. Next to the door, on the wall, I noticed an inset photograph of a man. A fair-haired man, with a handsome, lively face and dreamy eyes.

'Richard Wall . . . An American friend . . . Also murdered . . . '

He stood motionless before me, bowed.

'And there were others,' he whispered . . . 'Many others . . . If I were to add them up . . . All those dead . . . '

He opened the door for me. He seemed so distressed that I embraced him.

'Don't worry, old chap,' I said.

'You'll come and see me again, won't you? I feel so alone . . . And I'm frightened . . . '

'I'll come back.'

'And above all, read Alec's book . . . '

I plucked up my courage.

'I wonder . . . please . . . Would you print a few photographs for me . . . of Denise Coudreuse?'

'Of course. Anything you want . . . Don't lose the photos of Alec. And take care in the street . . . '

He closed the door and I heard him sliding the bolts home one after the other. I stood for a moment on the landing. I imagined him walking back along the dark blue corridor, into the drawing-room with its pink and green satins. And there, I was sure he would pick up the telephone, dial the number again, press the receiver feverishly to his ear, and listen tremulously, without tiring, to the faint messages of 'Blue Rider'.

21

We had left very early, that morning, in Denise's convertible and I believe we took the Porte de Saint-Cloud road. The sun must have been shining because Denise had on a large straw hat.

We reached a village in Seine-et-Oise or Seine-et-Marne and turned down a gently sloping, tree-lined street. Denise parked the car before a white gate which led into a garden. She pushed open the gate and I waited for her on the pavement outside.

A weeping willow, in the centre of the garden, and at the far end, a bungalow.

She returned with a little girl of about ten whose hair was fair and who was wearing a grey skirt. All three of us got into the car, the little girl in the back and I next to Denise, who drove. I no longer remember where we ate.

But in the afternoon we went for a walk in the grounds of Versailles and took a boat out with the little girl. The reflection of the sun on the water dazzled me. Denise lent me her sun glasses.

Later, the three of us were seated at a table with a sunshade and the little girl was eating a green and pink ice-cream. Around us, a large number of people in summer clothes. An orchestra playing. We brought the little girl back as night was falling. Crossing the town, we passed a fair and stopped.

I can see the wide, empty road at dusk and Denise and the little girl in a purple Dodgem which left a wake of sparks behind it. They were laughing and the little girl waved to me. Who was she?

22

That evening, sitting in the Agency, I studied the photographs Mansoure had given me.

A fat man, seated in the middle of a settee. He is wearing a silk dressing-gown, embroidered with flowers. A cigarette-holder between thumb and forefinger of the right hand. With his left hand, he is holding down the pages of a book, which rests on his knee. He is bald, his eyebrows are bushy, and his eyelids are lowered. He is reading. The short, thick nose, the grim fold of the mouth, the heavy oriental face, remind one of a bull-terrier. Above him, the carved wooden angel I had noticed on the cover of the magazine, behind Denise Coudreuse.

The second photo shows him standing up, wearing a double-breasted white suit, striped shirt and a dark tie. His left hand clasps a knobstick. His right arm, folded across his chest, and his hand, half open, lend him an affected air. He holds himself very stiffly, standing almost on tiptoe in his two-tone shoes. Gradually he detaches himself from the photo, comes to life, and I see him walking down a boulevard, under the trees, and limping.

23

Subject: SCOUFFI, Alexander.
Born in: Alexandria (Egypt), 28th April 1885.
Nationality: Greek.
Alexander Scouffi first came to France in 1920.
He has resided successively at:
    26, Rue de Naples, Paris 8
    11, Rue de Berne, Paris 8, in a furnished apartment
    Hôtel de Chicago, 99 Rue de Rome, Paris 17
    97, Rue de Rome, Paris 17, 5th floor.

Scouffi was a man of letters who published numerous articles in various periodicals, poems of all kinds and two novels: *At the Golden Fish Residential Hotel* and *Ship at Anchor.*

He also studied singing and although he did not work as a professional concert performer, he did make an appearance at the Salle Pleyel and the Théatre de la Monnaie in Brussels. In Paris, Scouffi attracted the attention of the Vice Squad. Regarded as an undesirable, his deportation was even considered.

In November 1924, when he was living at 26, Rue de Naples, he was questioned by the police in connection with an attempt to commit an offence against a minor. From November 1930 until September 1931, he lived in the Hôtel de Chicago, 99 Rue de Rome, with a young man, Pierre D, twenty years old, a soldier in the 8th Engineer Corps at Versailles. Evidently, Scouffi frequented the homosexual bars of Montmartre. Scouffi had a large income which came to him from property he had inherited from his father, in Egypt.

Murdered in his bachelor's flat, 97, Rue de Rome. The murderer was never found.

Subject: DE WRÉDÉ, Oleg.
AUTeuil 54-73

It has so far been impossible to identify the person
  bearing this name.
  It may be a pseudonym or an assumed name.
  Or it may belong to a foreign national who stayed only
  a short while in France.
The phone number AUTeuil 54-73 has not been
  assigned to anyone since 1952. For ten years, from
  1942 to 1952, it was assigned to:

THE COMET GARAGE

5, Rue Foucauld, Paris XVIth

This garage has been closed since 1952 and is shortly to
  be replaced by a block of flats.

A few words, appended to this typewritten sheet:
  'This is all the information I have been able to gather.
If you need more information, do not hesitate to ask.
And please convey my best wishes to Hutte.

Yours, Jean-Pierre Bernardy.'

24

But why does my clouded mind retain the image of
Scouffi, this fat man with his bulldog face, rather than
anyone else? Perhaps because of the white suit. A bright
spot, like a burst of orchestral music or the pure sound
of a voice amid the crackling and interferences when
you turn the knob of a radio . . .

I remember the bright patch made by this suit on the
stairs, and the dull tap-tap of the knobstick against the
steps. He used to stop at each landing. I passed him

several times when I was going up to Denise's apartment. I have a clear vision of the brass hand-rail, the beige-coloured wall, the dark wood, double doors of the apartments. The glow of a night light on each floor and this head, the gentle, sad look of a bulldog emerging from the shadows . . . I believe he even greeted me as we passed each other.

A café, at the corner of the Rue de Rome and the Boulevard des Batignolles. Summer, the terrace spills over on to the pavement and I am seated at one of the tables. It is evening. I am waiting for Denise. The last rays of the sun linger on the façade and the glass-fronted doors of the garage, over there, on the other side of the Rue de Rome, by the railway track . . .

Suddenly, I see him crossing the boulevard.

He is wearing his white suit and holding his knobstick in his right hand. He limps slightly. He moves off in the direction of the Place Clichy and my gaze follows this stiff, white figure, under the trees. It grows smaller and smaller and finally disappears. Then I sip some menthe-à-l'eau and speculate about what he is up to. What appointment is he keeping?

Denise was often late. She worked – it is all coming back to me now, thanks to that white figure moving off down the boulevard – she worked for a dressmaker, in the Rue la Boétie, a thin, fair-haired fellow who caused quite a stir later and who at the time was just starting out. I remember his first name, Jacques, and if I persevere, I shall certainly find his name in the old directories in Hutte's office. Rue la Boétie . . .

Night had already fallen when she joined me on the terrace of the café, but it did not bother me, I could have stayed there much longer in front of my menthe-à-l'eau. I preferred waiting on this terrace than in Denise's little apartment, which was quite near by. Nine o'clock. He crossed the boulevard, as was his habit. His suit seemed phosphorescent. Denise and he exchanged a few words, one evening, under the trees. The dazzling white suit, the swarthy bulldog face, the electric green foliage, had something summery and unreal about them.

Denise and I went in the opposite direction to him and followed the Boulevard de Courcelles. The Paris which we walked in at that time was as summery and unreal as Scouffi's phosphorescent suit. We floated in a night scented by privet as we passed the railings of the Parc Monceau. Very few cars. Red and green traffic lights lit up softly, for nothing, and these alternating colours were as gentle and rhythmic as the swaying of palm-trees.

Almost at the end of the Avenue Hoche, on the left, before the Place de l'Étoile, the large windows on the first floor of the town-house which had belonged to Sir Basil Zaharoff were always lit up. Later – or, perhaps, at the same period – I often went up to the first floor of this town-house: offices and a large crowd always. Groups of people talking, others telephoning feverishly. A continual coming-and-going. And no one ever even took off his coat. Why are certain things from the past recalled in such photographic detail?

We dined in a Basque restaurant, near the Avenue Victor-Hugo. Last night, I tried to find it again but failed. And yet I searched the whole district. It was on the corner of two very quiet streets and in front of it was a terrace, protected by tubs of greenery and a large red and green awning. Lots of people. I can hear the hum of conversation, the clink of glasses, I can see the mahogany bar inside, above which is a long fresco depicting a Gascony coast scene. I can still remember some of the faces. The tall, slender, fair-haired fellow at whose establishment in the Rue la Boétie Denise worked, and who sat down for a minute at our table. A dark man with a moustache, a red-haired woman, another man, with fair, curly hair this time, who laughed continuously. But unfortunately I cannot match these faces with names . . . The bald skull of the barman fixing a cocktail which he alone knew how to do. If I could only remember the name of this cocktail which was also the restaurant's name, it would awaken other memories, but how? Last night, wandering through these streets, I knew they were the same ones and I did not recognize them. The buildings had not changed, or the width of the pavements, but in that earlier time the light was different and there was something else in the air . . .

We returned by the same route. Often, we went to the cinema, a local picture house which I found again: the Royal-Villiers, Place de Lévis. It was the square with its benches, the Morris Column and the trees which recalled the spot to me, much more than the front of the cinema.

If I could remember the films we saw, I would be able to identify the time exactly, but only some vague impressions remain of them: a sledge sliding over the snow; a man in a dinner-jacket entering the cabin of a liner; silhouettes dancing behind french windows . . .

We were back in the Rue de Rome. Last night, I walked as far as number 97 and I believe I had the same feeling of distress as I had that earlier time, seeing the railings, the railway line, and opposite this the DUBONNET advertisement covering the whole wall of one of the buildings and whose colours had certainly faded since.

Number 99, the Hôtel de Chicago, was no longer called Hôtel 'de Chicago', but no one at the reception desk was able to tell me when it had changed its name. A fact of no importance.

Number 97 is a very large building. If Scouffi lived on the fifth floor, Denise's apartment was below, on the fourth. Was it the right or left side of the building? There were at least a dozen windows per floor, so that each floor was no doubt divided into one, two or three apartments. I studied the façade for a long time in the hope of recognizing a balcony, the shape or the shutters of a window. No, it did not remind me of anything.

Neither does the staircase. The hand-rail is not that brass one that shines in my memory. The doors to the apartments are not dark wood. And above all, the landing light with the time-switch does not produce that dim glow out of which Scouffi's strange, bulldog face would emerge. It was no use questioning the care-taker. She would be suspicious, and besides, caretakers change, like everything else.

Was Denise still living here when Scouffi was murdered? An event as tragic as this must surely have left some trace, if we had lived through it on the floor below. Not a trace of it in my memory. Denise could not have stayed long at 97, Rue de Rome, perhaps a few months. Did I live with her? Or did I have a place some-where else in Paris?

I remember a night when we came home very late. Scouffi was sitting on one of the steps of the staircase. His hands were folded about the top of his knobstick and his chin rested on his hands. The features of his face sagged, his bulldog look was stamped with distress. We stopped in front of him. He did not see us. We would have liked to speak to him, to help him up to his apartment, but he was still as a wax figure. The light went out and all that was left of him was the white, phosphorescent patch of his suit.

All this must have been at the beginning, when Denise and I had just met.

25

I turned off the light, but instead of leaving Hutte's office, I remained a few moments in the dark. Then I turned the light on again, and turned it off again. A third time, I turned on the light. And off. Something was stirring in me: I saw myself turning off the light in a room the size of this one, at some indeterminate period. And I did this every evening, at the same time.

The street lamp in the Avenue Niel makes the wood of Hutte's desk and armchair glow. In that other time too, I used to stand motionless for a few moments after having switched off the light, as though I was apprehensive about going out. There was a glass-fronted bookcase against the back wall, a grey marble mantelpiece with a mirror above it, a desk with numerous drawers and a settee, near the window, where I often lay down to read. The window looked out on to a silent street, lined with trees.

It was a small town-house, which served as premises for a South American legation. I no longer remember in what capacity I occupied an office of this legation. A man and a woman I hardly ever saw were in other offices next to mine and I used to hear them typing.

Very occasionally I would see people who wanted visas. It came back to me suddenly as I rummaged in the biscuit box which the Valbreuse gardener had given me and studied the Dominican Republic passport and the photographs. But I was acting for someone else, whose office I was using. A consul? A chargé d'affaires? I have not forgotten that I used to phone him for instructions. Who was he?

And first of all, where was his legation? For several days, I walked the XVIth arrondissement, since the silent, tree-lined street I saw in my mind's eye resembled the streets in this district. I was like a water-diviner watching for the slightest movement of his pendulum. At the top of each street I would stop, hoping that the trees, the buildings, would make me suddenly remember. I thought I felt something at the intersection of the Rue Molitor and the Rue Mirabeau and I had the sudden conviction that each evening, when I left the legation, this was the locality I found myself in.

It was night. Walking down the corridor which led to the staircase, I heard the sound of typing and stuck my head through the opening in the door. The man had already left and she was alone, sitting at her typewriter. I said good evening to her. She stopped typing and turned around. A pretty, dark-haired girl whose tropical looks I remember. She said something to me in Spanish, smiled and continued with her work. After standing awhile in the lobby, I finally decided to leave.

And I am certain that I am walking down the Rue Mirabeau, so straight, so dark, so deserted that I walk faster and am afraid that being the sole pedestrian, I shall be noticed. In the square, lower down, at the intersection with the Avenue de Versailles, a café is still lit up.

Sometimes I would choose the opposite route and plunge into the quiet streets of Auteuil. There I felt safe, coming out into the Chaussée de la Muette. I remember the tall buildings of the Boulevard Émile-Augier and the street to the right which I took. On the ground floor, a frosted-glass window, like a dentist's surgery, was always lit up. Denise waited for me a little further up, in a Russian restaurant.

I often mention bars or restaurants, but if it were not for a street or café sign from time to time, how would I ever find my way?

The restaurant extended into a walled garden. Through a bay, one could see the interior with its red velvet hangings. It was still day when we sat down at one of the garden tables. There was a zither player. The sound of this instrument, the evening light in the garden and the scent of foliage coming, no doubt, from the woods nearby, were all part of the mystery and the melancholy of that time. I tried to find the Russian restaurant again. No luck. The Rue Mirabeau has not changed, though. On the evenings I stayed later at the legation, I used to continue along the Avenue de Versailles. I could have taken the Métro but I preferred to walk in the open air. Quai de Passy. Pont de Bir-Hakeim. Then the Avenue de New-York, along which I walked the other night with Waldo Blunt, and now I understand why my heart missed a beat. Without realizing it, I was retracing my steps. How many times had I walked along the Avenue de New-York . . . Place de l'Alma, the first oasis. Then the trees and the coolness of the Cours-la-Reine. After crossing the Place de la Concorde, I've almost reached my goal. Rue Royale. I turn right, Rue Saint-Honoré. Left, Rue Cambon.

Not a light in the Rue Cambon, except for a bluish reflection which must come from a shop window. My footsteps echo on the pavement. I am alone. Again fear seizes me, the fear I feel each time I walk down the Rue Mirabeau, the fear that I shall be noticed, stopped, and that they will ask for my papers. It would be a pity, just a few yards from my destination. Above all, not to run. Walk right to the end, at a steady pace.

The Hôtel Castille. I pass through the door. There is no one at the reception desk. I walk into the morning-room, long enough to recover my breath and wipe the sweat from my brow. This night too I have escaped danger. She is waiting for me up there. She is the only one to wait for me, the only one in this town who would be concerned if I vanished.

A room with light green walls. The red curtains are drawn. The light comes from a bedside lamp, to the left of the bed. I smell her perfume, a pungent scent, and all I see now is the whiteness of her skin and the beauty spot above her right buttock.

26

He would return from the beach with his son, at about seven in the evening. This was the time of day he liked best. He held the child by the hand or else let him run on ahead.

The avenue was deserted, a few rays of sunlight lingered on the pavement. They walked through the arcade and the child stopped every time in front of the confectioners, Queen Astrid's. He, for his part, looked in the window of the bookshop.

That evening, a book in the window attracted his attention. The title, in garnet lettering, included the word 'Castille' and while he walked under the arcade, holding his son's hand, and the latter enjoyed himself leaping the rays of sunlight which striped the pavement, the word 'Castille' reminded him of a hotel, in Paris, near the Faubourg Saint-Honoré.

Once, a man had arranged to see him at the Hôtel Castille. They had already met in the Avenue Hoche offices, among all the strange people who discussed their affairs in low voices, and the man had proposed selling him a clip and two diamond bracelets, as he wanted to leave France. He had entrusted him with the diamonds, in a small leather case, and they had agreed to meet again the next evening at the Hôtel Castille, where the man lived.

The hotel reception desk came back to him, the tiny bar next to it, and the walled garden with its green trellises. The porter phoned up to announce his arrival, then told him the room number.

The man was stretched out on the bed, a cigarette between his lips. He was not inhaling the smoke but puffed it out nervously in dense clouds. A tall, dark-skinned man, who had introduced himself the day before, at the Avenue Hoche, as the 'former commercial attaché of a South American legation'. He had told him only his first name: Pedro.

The man 'Pedro' had sat up on the edge of the bed and given him a shy smile. He did not know why he felt drawn to him without knowing him. In this hotel room, 'Pedro' seemed like a hunted animal. He immediately handed him the envelope with the money. The day before he had managed to sell the stones for a large profit. Here you are, he said, I've added half the profit for you. 'Pedro' thanked him, putting the envelope away in the drawer of his night-table.

At that moment, he had noticed that one of the doors of the wardrobe facing the bed was half open. Dresses and a fur coat were hanging there. So, 'Pedro' was living here with a woman. Again he thought that their situation, 'Pedro's' and this woman's, must be precarious.

Stretched out on the bed again, 'Pedro' lit another cigarette. He must have felt he could trust him, because he said:

'I'm more and more scared of going out . . . '

And he had even added:

'Some days I'm so afraid, I stay in bed . . . '

After all this time, he could still hear these two sentences spoken by 'Pedro' in his low voice. He had not known what to answer. He made some general comment, like: 'Strange times we live in.'

Then Pedro, suddenly said to him:

'I think I've found a way of getting out of France . . . With money, everything's possible . . . '

He remembered that tiny snowflakes – almost rain-drops – were swirling outside the window. And this snow, the night outside, the bareness of the room, made him feel he was suffocating. Was it still possible to get away, even with money?

'Yes,' whispered Pedro . . . 'I know how to get into Portugal . . . Through Switzerland . . . '

The word 'Portugal' had immediately conjured up the

green ocean, the sun, an orange-coloured drink which one sipped through a straw, seated under an umbrella. And what if he and this 'Pedro' were to meet again one day, he had said to himself, in summer, in a café in Lisbon or Estoril? Nonchalantly they would squeeze the soda-syphon nozzle . . . How distant it would all seem to them then, this little room in the Hôtel Castille, the snow, the dark, the gloom of this Paris winter which it was so difficult to escape . . . He had left the room, saying 'Good luck' to 'Pedro'.

What became of 'Pedro'? He hoped that this man whom he had met only twice, so long ago, was as untroubled, as happy as he was himself this summer evening, with a child who stepped over the last patches of sunlight on the pavement.

27

My dear Guy, thank you for your letter. I am very happy in Nice. I have found the old Russian church in the Rue Longchamp where my grandmother often took me. That was the time, too, when my passion for tennis was awakened by seeing King Gustav of Sweden play . . . In Nice, every street corner reminds me of my childhood.

In the Russian church I am speaking of, there is a room lined with glass-fronted book-cases. In the middle of this room, a large table which looks like a billiard-table, and some old armchairs. This is where my grandmother came every Wednesday to borrow a few books, and I always accompanied her.

The books date from the end of the nineteenth century. And, besides, the place has kept the charm of reading-rooms of that period. I spend a lot of time there reading Russian, which I had forgotten a little.

Outside the church is a shady garden, with large palm-trees and eucalyptuses. Amid this tropical vegetation, is a birch tree with a silvery trunk. It was planted there, I suppose, to remind us of our distant Russia.

Dare I confess it, Guy – I have applied for the position of librarian? If it works out, as I hope it will, I shall be delighted to receive you in one of my childhood haunts.

After many vicissitudes (I have not had the courage to tell the priest that I was a private detective by profession), I am returning to my roots.

You were right to tell me that in life it is not the future which counts, but the past.

As regards what you have asked me, the best thing, I think, would be to apply to De Swert's agency, 'In the family interest'. I have, therefore, written to him, as he is, I believe, well placed to answer your question. He will send you information very promptly.

Yours,

Hutte

P.S. As regards the so-called 'Oleg de Wrédé', whom we have not yet been able to identify, I have some good news: you will receive a letter in the next post, which will give you information about him. As a matter of fact, I questioned some old members of the Russian colony in Nice, at random, thinking that 'Wrédé' had a Russian – or Baltic – sound to it, and by chance I came across a Mrs Kahan, for whom this name held certain memories. Bad memories, as it turns out, which she would rather forget, but she promised me to write to you and tell you all she knew.

Subject: COUDREUSE, Denise, Yvette.
Born at: Paris, 21st December, 1917, to Paul COUDREUSE and Henriette, née BOGAERTS.
Nationality: French.
Married, 3rd April, 1939 at the town-hall of the XVIIth arrondissement to Jimmy Pedro Stern, born 30th September, 1912 in Salonica (Greece), of Greek nationality.

Miss Coudreuse has resided successively:
9, Quai d'Austerlitz, Paris 13
97, Rue de Rome, Paris 17
Hôtel Castille, Rue Cambon, Paris 8
10A, Rue Cambacérès, Paris 8

Miss Coudreuse modelled for fashion photographs under the name of 'Muth'. After this, she worked evidently for the dress designer, JF, 32, Rue la Boétie, as a mannequin; then she was associated with a certain Van Allen, a Dutch subject, who, in April 1941, opened a fashion house at 6, Square de l'Opéra, Paris 9. The latter establishment was short-lived and closed in January 1945.

Miss Coudreuse disappeared while attempting to cross the Franco-Swiss border clandestinely, in February 1943. Investigations pursued in Megève (Haute-Savoie) and Annemasse (Haute-Savoie) have yielded no results.

29

Subject: STERN, Jimmy, Pedro.
Born at: Salonica (Greece), 30th September, 1912, to George STERN and Giuvia SARANO.
Nationality: Greek.
Married, 3rd April 1939, at the town-hall of the XVIIth arrondissement to Denise Yvette Coudreuse, of French nationality.
It is not known where Mr Stern resided in France.
A single form, dating from February 1939, indicates that a Mr Jimmy Pedro Stern lived at that time at:
Hôtel Lincoln
24, Rue Bayard, Paris 8.
This is, moreover, the address which appears on the marriage certificate issued at the town-hall of the XVIIth arrondissement.
The registration form of the Hôtel Lincoln contained the following:
Name: STERN, Jimmy, Pedro.
Address: Via delle Botteghe Oscure, 2 Rome (Italy).
Profession: broker.
Mr Jimmy Stern seems to have disappeared in 1940.

30

Subject: MCEVOY, Pedro.
It has been very hard to find any information about Mr Pedro McEvoy, either at police headquarters or at the general information bureau. It has been reported to us that a Mr Pedro McEvoy, a Dominican subject, and

working at the Dominican Legation in Paris, resided,
in December 1940, at 9, Rue Julien-Potin, at Neuilly
(Seine).
After that, we lose sight of him.
In all probability, Mr Pedro McEvoy left France before
the last war.
He may also be a person using an assumed name and
carrying false papers, as was common at the time.

31

It was Denise's birthday. A winter evening, with the
snow falling on Paris turning to slush. People were
swallowed up by Métro entrances and walked briskly.
The shop windows of the Faubourg Saint-Honoré were
lit up. Christmas was approaching.

I went into a jeweller's, and I can still see the man's
face. He had a beard and wore tinted glasses. I bought a
ring for Denise. When I left the shop, the snow was still
falling. I was afraid Denise would not be at our meeting
place and for the first time it occurred to me that we
might lose each other in this town, among all these
hurrying shadows.

And I no longer remember if, that evening, my name
was Jimmy or Pedro, Stern or McEvoy.

32

Valparaiso. She is standing, at the back of the tram, near
the window, in the crush of passengers, squeezed

between a little man with dark glasses and a dark-haired woman with the head of a mummy, who gives off a scent of violets.

Soon nearly all of them will get off at the Plaza Echaurren and she will be able to sit down. She comes into Valparaiso only twice a week to do her shopping, since she lives on the heights of the Cerro Alegre district. She rents a house there, in which she has set up her dancing school.

She does not regret having left Paris, five years ago now, after breaking her ankle, when she knew she would never dance again. She decided to leave then, to cut all ties with what had been her life. Why Valparaiso? Because she knew someone there, a former member of Cuevas's ballet.

She no longer expects to return to Europe. She will remain up there, giving her lessons, and will finally forget the old photographs of herself on the walls, dating from when she was a member of Colonel de Basil's company.

She only occasionally thinks of her life before the accident. Everything is confused in her mind. She mixes up names, dates, places. And yet, one memory returns to her regularly, twice a week, at the same time and same place, a memory more vivid than the others. It is when the tram stops, as now, at the bottom of the Avenida Errazuriz. This shady Avenue, sloping gently upwards, reminds her of the Rue Jouy-en-Josas, where she lived as a child. She can still see the house, on the corner of the Rue du Docteur-Kurzenne, the weeping willow, the white gate, the Protestant church below, and right at the bottom, the Robin Hood Inn. She remembers a Sunday, different from the others. Her godmother had come to fetch her.

She knows nothing about this woman, except her first name: Denise. She had a convertible. That Sunday, a dark-skinned man accompanied her. All three of them had gone to have an ice-cream and they had taken a boat out, and in the evening, when they left Versailles to take her back to Jouy-en-Josas, they had stopped at a fair. She and her godmother, Denise, had climbed into a Dodgem, while the dark-skinned man watched.

She would have liked to have known more about it. What were their names? Where did they live? What had happened to them after all this time? These were the questions she asked herself as the tram continued along the Avenida Errazuriz, climbing towards the Cerro Alegre district.

33

That evening, I was sitting at a table in the bar-cum-greengrocers to which Hutte had introduced me and which was situated on the Avenue Niel, just opposite the Agency. A counter and, on the shelves, exotic food products: teas, Turkish delight, rose-petal preserves, Baltic herrings. The place was frequented by ex-jockeys, talking over old times and showing each other dog-eared photographs of horses whose carcasses had long ago been cut up for meat.

Two men, at the bar, were speaking under their breath. One of them was wearing an overcoat which was the colour of dead leaves, and reached down almost to his ankles. He was short, like most of the customers. He turned round, no doubt to see what time the clock over the entrance showed, and his gaze fell on me.

His face grew very pale. His mouth hung open and his eyes stared.

He approached me slowly, frowning. He stopped at my table.

'Pedro.'

He fingered the material of my jacket, at the height of my biceps.

'Pedro, it's you?'

I hesitated before answering. He seemed put out.

'Excuse me,' he said. 'But aren't you Pedro McEvoy?'

'Yes,' I said shortly. 'Why?'

'Pedro, you . . . you don't recognize me?'

'No.'

He sat down opposite me.

'Pedro . . . I'm . . . André Wildmer . . . '

He was upset. He took my hand.

'André Wildmer . . . The jockey . . . Don't you remember me?'

'I'm sorry,' I said. 'There are gaps in my memory. When did we meet?'

'But you must know . . . Freddie and I . . . '

This name had the effect of an electric shock on me. A jockey. The gardener at Valbreuse had spoken to me of a jockey.

'That's funny,' I said. 'Someone spoke to me about you . . . At Valbreuse . . . '

His eyes misted over. The drink? Or was it emotion?

'Oh, come on, Pedro . . . Don't you remember when the three of us, you, me, and Freddie, used to go to Valbreuse? . . . '

'Not too well. But it was the gardener at Valbreuse who spoke to me about it . . . '

'Pedro . . . So you're alive, you're alive?'

He clasped my hand very tight. It hurt.

'Yes. Why?'

'You're . . . you're in Paris?'

'Yes. Why?'

He looked at me in horror. He had trouble believing that I was alive. So, what had happened? I wanted to know, but apparently he did not dare tackle this question head on.

'I . . . live at Giverny . . . in the Oise,' he said. 'I . . . I very rarely come to Paris . . . Would you like a drink, Pedro?'

'A Marie Brizard,' I said.

'I'll have one too.'

He poured the drink himself into our glasses, slowly, and he seemed to me to be playing for time.

'Pedro . . . What happened?'

'When?'

He finished his drink at one gulp.

'When you tried to get over the Swiss frontier with Denise? . . . '

What could I answer?

'You never sent us any news. Freddie was very worried . . . '

He filled his glass again.

'We thought you'd got lost in all that snow . . . '

'You shouldn't have worried,' I said.

'And Denise?'

I shrugged.

'Do you remember Denise well?' I asked.

'But Pedro, of course I do . . . And anyway, why are you being so formal with me?'

'I'm sorry, old man,' I said. 'I haven't been too well lately. I'm trying to remember that whole period . . . But it's so hazy . . . '

'I know. It's a long time ago, all that . . . Do you remember Freddie's wedding?'

He smiled.

'Not too well.'

'In Nice . . . When he married Gay . . . '

'Gay Orlov?'

'Of course, Gay Orlov . . . Whom else would he have married?'

He looked very upset that this marriage no longer conveyed much to me.

'In Nice . . . The Russian church . . . A religious ceremony . . . No civil marriage . . . '

'What Russian church?'

'A little Russian church with a garden . . . '

Was it the one Hutte described in his letter? Sometimes there are the oddest coincidences.

'Yes, of course,' I said . . . 'Of course . . . The little Russian church in the Rue Longchamp, with the garden and the library . . . '

'So, you remember? We were the four witnesses . . . We held crowns over Freddie's and Gay's heads . . . '

'Four witnesses?'

'Yes . . . you, me, Gay's grandfather . . . '

'Old Giorgiadze? . . . '

'That's it . . . Giorgiadze . . . '

The photograph where I appeared together with Gay Orlov and old Giorgiadze must have been taken on that occasion. I would show him it.

'And the fourth witness was your friend Rubirosa . . . '

'Who?'

'Your friend Rubirosa . . . Porfirio . . . The Dominican diplomat . . . '

He smiled at the memory of this Porfirio Rubirosa. A Dominican diplomat. Maybe he was the one I worked for at the legation.

'Afterwards we went to old Giorgiadze's . . . '

I could see us, around midday, walking along an avenue lined with plane-trees, in Nice. The sun shone.

'And was Denise there?'

He shrugged.

'Of course she was . . . You certainly have forgotten it all . . . '

The seven of us walked carelessly along, the jockey, Denise, I, Gay Orlov and Freddie, Rubirosa and the old Giorgiadze. We were wearing white suits.

'Giorgiadze lived in the apartment building on the corner of the Alsace-Lorraine Gardens.'

Palm-trees rising high into the sky. And children tobogganing. The white façade of the building, with its orange, canvas blinds. Our laughter on the staircase.

'That evening, your friend Rubirosa took us out to dinner at Eden Rock, to celebrate the marriage . . . So . . . do you remember now? . . . '

He breathed hard, as though he had just exerted

himself physically. He seemed exhausted by the effort to call to mind that day when Freddie and Gay Orlov got married in church, that day of sun and carefreeness, which no doubt had been one of those privileged moments of youth.

'In fact,' I said, 'you and I have known each other a long time then . . . '

'Yes . . . But I knew Freddie first . . . Because I was his grandfather's jockey . . . Unfortunately, it didn't last long . . . The old man lost everything . . . '

'And Gay Orlov . . . Do you know that . . . '

'Yes, I know . . . I lived quite close to her . . . Square des Aliscamps . . . '

The large apartment building and the windows from which Gay Orlov must have had a fine view of the Auteuil race course. Waldo Blunt, her first husband, had told me that she killed herself because she was afraid of growing old. I suppose that she often watched the races from her window. Each day, several times in the afternoon, ten or so horses leap forward, fly over the course and smash into obstacles. And those which jump them are seen again for several months and then they too vanish like the others. New horses are needed constantly, and are progressively replaced. And each time the same burst of energy ends in disaster . . . Such a spectacle cannot fail to depress and disenchant and it was perhaps because she lived next to a race course that Gay Orlov . . . I felt like asking André Wildmer what he thought of this. He should understand. He was a jockey.

'It's really sad,' he said. 'Gay was a real brick . . . '

He leant forward and brought his face up close to mine. His skin was red and pock-marked and he had dark brown eyes. There was a transversal scar across his right cheek which extended as far as the point of his chin. His hair, too, was brown, except for a white streak over his brow.

'And you, Pedro . . . '

122

But I did not let him finish his sentence.

'Did you know me when I lived in the Rue Julien-Potin, at Neuilly?' I said on the off chance, remembering the address on 'Pedro McEvoy's' form.

'When you lived at Rubirosa's . . . Of course . . . '

Rubirosa again.

'Freddie and I often came . . . It was high jinks every night . . . '

He burst out laughing.

'Your friend Rubirosa used to hire musicians . . . it went on all night . . . Do you remember those two tunes he always played on the guitar?'

'No . . . '

'"El Reloj" and "Tu me acostumbraste". Especially "Tu me acostumbraste" . . . '

He whistled a few bars of the tune.

'Well?'

'Yes . . . yes . . . It's coming back,' I said.

'You got me a Dominican passport . . . It wasn't much use to me . . . '

'You'd already been to see me at the legation?' I asked.

'Yes . . . When you gave me the Dominican passport.'

'I never understood what I was supposed to be doing at that legation.'

'I don't know . . . You told me once that you acted more or less as Rubirosa's secretary and that it was a good spot for you . . . It was sad that Rubi got himself killed in that car accident . . . '

Yes, sad. Another witness I would not be able to question.

'Tell me, Pedro . . . What was your real name? It always intrigued me. Freddie told me your name wasn't Pedro McEvoy . . . But that it was Rubi who had got you false papers . . . '

'My real name? I wish I knew.'

And I smiled, so that he could take it as a joke.

'Freddie knew it, since you were school friends . . .
You would drive me crazy with your stories about Luiza
College . . . '

'What college?'

'Luiza . . . You know perfectly well . . . Don't play
games . . . That day your father came to fetch the two of
you by car . . . He let Freddie drive, though he didn't
have a licence yet . . . You told me the story at least a
hundred times . . . '

He shook his head. So, I had had a father who came to
fetch me at 'Luiza College'. An interesting piece of
information.

'And you?' I said. 'Do you still work with horses?'

'I've found a job as instructor in a riding-school at
Giverny . . . '

His voice had taken on a solemn tone which impressed itself forcefully on me.

'As you know, from the time of my accident it's been
downhill . . . '

What accident? I did not dare ask him . . .

'When I accompanied you, Denise, Freddie and Gay
to Megève, things were already not going too well . . .
I'd lost my trainer's job . . . They got into a funk
because I was English . . . They only wanted French . . . '

English? Yes. He spoke with a slight accent that I had
hardly noticed up to then. My heart started beating a
little harder when he uttered the word: Megève.

'A funny idea, don't you think, that journey to
Megève,' I ventured.

'Why funny? What else could we have done? . . . '

'You think so?'

'It was a safe place . . . Paris was getting too dangerous . . . '

'Do you really think so?'

'But Pedro, just remember . . . There were checks
more and more often . . . I was English . . . Freddie
had an English passport . . . '

'English?'

'Of course . . . Freddie's family was from Mauritius . . . And your position wasn't too wonderful either . . . And our bogus Dominican passports couldn't really protect us any longer . . . Just remember . . . Your friend Rubirosa himself . . . '

I could not catch the rest of his sentence. I think he suffered a loss of voice.

He sipped his drink and at that moment four people came in, regular customers, all of them ex-jockeys. I recognized them, I had often heard them talking. One of them still wore an old pair of riding breeches and a suede jacket stained all over. They tapped Wildmer on the shoulder. They were all speaking at once, roaring with laughter, and it made much too much noise. Wildmer did not introduce them to me.

They sat down on barstools and continued talking in very loud voices.

'Pedro . . . '

Wildmer leant towards me. His face was only a few inches from mine. He grimaced as though he were about to make a superhuman effort to utter a few words.

'Pedro . . . What happened to Denise when you tried to cross the border? . . . '

'I no longer know,' I said.

He looked at me fixedly. He must have been a bit drunk.

'Pedro . . . Before you left I told you you ought to be careful with that fellow . . . '

'What fellow?'

'The fellow who was going to get you across into Switzerland . . . The Russian with the face of a gigolo . . . '

He was purple-faced. He swallowed some of the liqueur.

'Don't you remember . . . I told you you shouldn't listen to that other one either . . . The ski instruc-tor . . . '

'What ski instructor?'

'The one who was going to be your guide . . . You know . . . That Bob something . . . Bob Besson . . . Why did you go? . . . You were all right with us at the chalet . . . '

What could I say to him? I nodded. He emptied his glass in a single gulp.

'His name was Bob Besson?' I asked.

'Yes, Bob Besson . . . '

'And the Russian?'

He frowned.

'I don't remember now . . . '

His concentration was going. He had made a mighty effort to speak to me of the past, but it was over. Just like an exhausted swimmer who raises his head a last time above the waves and then lets himself sink slowly . . . After all, I had not given him much help.

He rose and joined the others. He was slipping back into his routine. I heard him giving his opinion in a loud voice about a race which had taken place that afternoon at Vincennes. The man in riding breeches stood a round of drinks. Wildmer had found his voice again and was so vehement, so impassioned that he had forgotten to light his cigarete. It hung from his lips. If I had stood in front of him, he would not have recognized me now.

As I left, I said goodbye to him and waved, but he ignored me. He was completely taken up in what he was saying.

34

Vichy. An American car stops by the Parc des Sources, opposite the Hôtel de la Paix. Its bodywork is spattered with mud. Two men and a woman get out and walk towards the hotel entrance. The two men are unshaven and one of the two, the taller, holds the woman by the arm. In front of the hotel, a row of wicker armchairs in which people sleep, their heads lolling, seemingly indifferent to the July sun which beats down upon them.

In the hotel lounge, the three of them have difficulty making their way through to the reception desk. They have to walk around armchairs and even camp beds where other sleepers sprawl, some of them in military uniform. Tight little groups of five or ten people huddle in the lounge at the back, call out to each other, and the hubbub is even more oppressive than the heat and humidity outside. Finally they reach the desk, and one of the men, the taller, hands the porter their three passports. Two are passports issued by the Legation of the Dominican Republic in Paris, one in the name of 'Porfirio Rubirosa', the other in that of 'Pedro McEvoy'; the third is a French passport in the name of 'Denise, Yvette, Coudreuse'.

The porter, his face bathed in sweat which drips from his chin, returns their passports, with a helpless gesture. No, there is not a single free hotel room in the whole of Vichy, 'seeing how things are' . . . At a pinch, there might be a couple of armchairs which one might be able to take up to a laundry-room or put in a toilet on the ground floor . . . His voice is submerged in the confused hullabaloo of conversations, the metallic banging of the lift door, the ringing of the telephone, the messages coming over the loud-speaker hanging above the reception desk.

The two men and women have left the hotel, walking somewhat unsteadily. The sky has suddenly grown overcast, with purplish grey clouds. They cross the Parc des Sources. On the lawns, under the covered walks, obstructing the paved lanes, stand groups of people, huddling closer together even than in the hotel. They all talk in very loud voices among themselves, some people run to and fro between groups, others gather in twos or threes on a bench or on the park's iron seats, before rejoining the others . . . It looks like a huge school playground and one finds oneself waiting impatiently for the bell to put an end to all this agitation and to the din of voices swelling from moment to moment. But no bell sounds.

The tall, dark man still holds the woman by the arm, while the other one has taken off his jacket. They walk and are jostled as they go by people running in all directions to find some person or some group which they have left for a moment, which has instantly dissolved and whose members have been snapped up by other groups.

The three of them find themselves in front of the terrace of the Café de la Restauration. The terrace is packed, but by a miracle five people have just left one of the tables, and the two men and woman drop into the wicker chairs. Somewhat dazed, they look over towards the casino.

A haze has enveloped the entire park and the arching foliage keeps it from dissipating, making it stagnate there. It is like the steam in a Turkish bath. It invades your throat, finally it blurs the groups standing in front of the casino, it muffles the din of their voices. At a neighbouring table, an old lady bursts into sobs and says over and over that the frontier at Hendaye is closed.

The woman's head has topped over on to the tall, dark man's shoulder. She has closed her eyes. She sleeps like a child. The two men exchange smiles. Then, again, they look at all the groups in front of the casino.

There is a sudden shower. Monsoon rainfall. It penetrates the cover of plane-trees and chestnuts, in spite of the density of the foliage. Over there, people are jostling each other, seeking shelter under the casino's glass top, while others hastily leave the terrace and enter the café, trampling on each other.

Only the two men and the woman have not moved, as

the parasol over their table protects them from the rain. The woman still sleeps, her cheek resting on the tall, dark man's shoulder. He looks straight ahead vacantly, while his companion absentmindedly whistles the tune of: 'Tu me acostumbraste'.

35

From the window could be seen the expanse of lawn, with a gravel path skirting it. It sloped very gently upward towards the building where I was and which had reminded me of one of those white hotels on the shores of the Mediterranean. But when I had climbed the steps, my eyes had fallen on the inscription in silver lettering adorning the door: 'Luiza and Albany College'.

At the far end of the lawn, a tennis court. To the right, a row of birch trees and a swimming pool which had been emptied. The diving board had half collapsed.

He rejoined me in the window recess.

'Yes, as I thought . . . I am very sorry . . . All the college records were burnt . . . There is nothing left . . . '

A man of about sixty, who wore glasses with pale tortoise-shell frames and a tweed jacket.

'And in any case, Mrs Jeanschmidt would not have authorized it . . . Since her husband's death, she won't discuss Luiza College at all . . . '

'Aren't there any old class photographs around the place?' I asked.

'No. As I said, everything has been burnt . . . '

'Have you worked here long?'

'The two last years of Luiza College. Then, our

director, Mr Jeanschmidt, died . . . But the college was no longer the same as it used to be . . . '

He looked out of the window with a pensive air.

'As a former student, I'd have liked to find some souvenirs,' I said.

'I understand. Unfortunately . . . '

'And what will become of the college?'

'Oh, they'll auction everything off.'

And with a listless gesture, he took in the lawn, the tennis court, the swimming pool.

'Would you like a last look at the dormitories and the class rooms?'

'There's no point.'

He took a pipe from his jacket pocket and stuck it in his mouth. He did not leave the window recess.

'What was that wooden building on the left?'

'The changing rooms. They changed there for sport . . . '

'Oh, yes, that's right . . . '

He filled his pipe.

'I've forgotten everything . . . Did we wear a uniform?'

'No, sir. A navy-blue blazer was required for dinner only and on days out.'

I approached the window. My forehead practically touched the glass. Below, in front of the white building, was a gravel-covered esplanade, with weeds already coming through. I could see us, Freddie and me, in our blazers. And I tried to imagine what he might have looked like, that man who came for us on one of the days out, who left his car and walked towards us, who was my father.

36

Mrs E. Kahan
22, Rue de Picardie,
Nice.   Nice, 22nd November, 1965

I am writing to you, at Mr Hutte's request, to tell
you all I know about the man, 'Oleg de Wrédé', even
though to remember him is disagreeable for me.

One day I went into a Russian restaurant, in the
Rue Francois-1er, Chez Arkady, run by a Russian
gentleman whose name I no longer recall. It was a
modest restaurant, there were not many people there.
The manager, a man prematurely aged, unhappy and
sick-looking, stood at the zakuski table – this was
some time around 1937.

I became aware of the presence of a young man of
about twenty, who looked at home in this restaurant.
Too well dressed, suit, shirt, etc. – impeccable.

His appearance was striking: a vitality, narrow
china-blue eyes, a dazzling smile, always laughing.
And behind it, an animal cunning.

He was at the next table to mine. The second time
I came to the place, he pointed to the restaurant
manager and said:

'Would you believe I'm that gentleman's son?' with
a look of contempt for the poor old man who was, in
fact, his father.

Then he showed me an identity bracelet on which
was engraved the name: 'Louis de Wrédé, Comte de
Montpensier' (in the restaurant, he was called by the
Russian name: Oleg). I asked him where his mother
was. He told me she was dead. I asked him where on
earth she could have met a Montpensier (connected
with the younger branch of the house of Orléans, it

seems). He answered: In Siberia. None of this made any sense. I realised he was a little blackguard who preyed on people of both sexes. When I asked him what he did, he told me he played the piano.

Then began an enumeration of all his society connections – that the Duchess of Uzès was running after him, that he was on the best of terms with the Duke of Windsor . . . I felt there was both truth and falsehood in his stories. People in 'high society' were no doubt taken in by his 'name', his smile, his glacial but really quite engaging manner.

During the war – I think it was between '41 and '42 – I was on the beach at Juan-les-Pins when this man, 'Oleg de Wrédé', came running up, in his usual form and laughing heartily. He told me he had been a prisoner and that a high-ranking German officer was taking care of him. Just now, he was spending a few days with his self-appointed godmother, a Mrs Henri Duvernois, a widow. But he said: 'She's so mean, she won't give me any money.'

He announced that he was returning to Paris, 'to work with the Germans.' 'What at?' I asked. 'Selling them cars.'

I never saw him again and do not know what became of him. That, I am afraid, is all that I can tell you regarding this individual.

Respectfully yours,

E. Kahan

37

Now, all I need do is close my eyes. The events preceding our departure for Megève come back to me bit by bit. The large, brightly lit windows of the former

Zaharoff residence, in the Avenue Hoche, and Wildmer's disjointed sentences, and the names, like the purple, scintillating one of 'Rubirosa', and the pallid one of 'Oleg de Wrédé', as well as other less tangible details – the sound of Wildmer's voice, rough, so low you could barely hear him – all these things serve as my Ariadne's thread.

The day before, in the late afternoon, I found myself, as it happens, in the Avenue Hoche, on the first floor of Zaharoff's old mansion. A lot of people. As usual, they kept their coats on. I, for my part, was not wearing one. I crossed the main room, where I saw some fifteen people clustered about the telephones, or sitting in leather armchairs talking business, and slipped into a little office, closing the door behind me. The man I was supposed to meet was already there. He led me to a corner of the room and we sat down in two armchairs separated by a low table. I placed on it the gold 20-franc pieces wrapped in newspaper. He at once handed me several wads of bank notes which I did not bother to count and which I stuffed into my pocket. The jewellery did not interest him. We left the office together, then the large room where the hum of conversation and the coming-and-going of all these men in overcoats was somehow disturbing. In the street, he gave me the address of a possible buyer for the jewels, near the Place Malesherbes, and suggested I tell the woman that he had sent me. It was snowing, but I decided to go on foot. Denise and I had often walked this way in the early days. Times had changed. It was snowing and I could hardly recognize the boulevard, with its bare trees, the dark façades of its buildings. No more scent from the privet hedges by the railings of the Parc Monceau, but a smell of damp earth and decay.

A ground floor flat, at the end of a blind alley, the kind called 'villa' or 'square'. The room where she received me was unfurnished. Just the divan, where we sat, and a telephone on the divan. A woman in her

forties, nervous, red-haired. The telephone rang endlessly and she did not always answer, and when she did
answer, she noted down what was said to her in an
engagement book. I showed her the jewellery. I let her
have the clip and the diamond bracelet at half price, on
condition that she paid me on the spot. She agreed.

Outside, as I was walking towards the Courcelles
Métro station, I thought of that young man who had
come to our room in the Hôtel Castille, a few months
before. He had disposed of the sapphire and the two
brooches very quickly, and had very decently offered to
share the profit with me. A man of feeling. I confided in
him a little, telling him of my plans to leave and even of
that fear which sometimes stopped me going out. He
told me that we lived in strange times.

Later I went to fetch Denise, in the apartment, in the
Square Édouard-VII, where Van Allen, her Dutch
friend, had established his fashion house: it was on the
first floor of a building, over the Cintra. I remember,
because Denise and I used to frequent this bar, since its
cellar room allowed one to slip out through a different
exit. I think I knew all the public places, all the
buildings in Paris with two exits.

In this tiny fashion house, the agitation was similar to
that in the Avenue Hoche apartment, perhaps even
more feverish. Van Allen was preparing his summer
collection, and all these efforts, the optimism, impressed me, since I wondered if there were going to be
any more summers. He was trying a dress of some light,
white material on a dark-haired girl, while other
mannequins were going in and out of the changing
rooms. Several people were talking around a Louis XV
desk, on which were scattered sketches and fabric
samples. In a corner of the room, Denise was in
conversation with a blonde woman of about fifty and a
young man with curly brown hair. I joined them. They
were leaving, she and he, for the Côte d'Azur. In the

general hubbub, it was impossible to hear what was said. Glasses of champagne circulated, without anyone quite knowing why.

Denise and I pushed our way through to the lobby. Van Allen accompanied us. I can still see his very light, blue eyes and his smile when he poked his head through the opening of the door and blew us a kiss, wishing us good luck.

Denise and I paid a last visit to the Rue Cambacérès. We had already packed a case and two leather bags which were waiting by the large table, at the end of the drawing-room. Denise closed the shutters and drew the curtains. She covered the sewing machine and removed the white canvas cloth pinned to the dress-stand. I thought about the evenings we had spent here. She would follow the patterns Van Allen gave her, or sew, while I stretched out on the couch and read some memoirs or one of the detective novels in the 'Collection du Masque' series which she like so much. Those evenings were the only times I could relax, the only times when I could have the illusion that we were leading an uneventful life in a peaceful world.

I opened the case and slipped the wads of bank notes which bulged out my pockets in among the sweaters and shirts and deep inside a pair of shoes. Denise checked the contents of one of the bags to see whether she had forgotten anything. I went down the corridor to the bedroom. I did not switch on the light and stood at the window. The snow was still falling. A policeman on sentry duty, on the opposite pavement, stood inside a shelter which had been placed there a few days before, because it was winter. Another policeman, coming from the Place des Saussaies, hurried towards the shelter. He shook hands with his colleague, handed him a Thermos flask and they took turns drinking from the cup.

Denise entered the room. She joined me at the window. She was wearing a fur coat and stood close to me. She smelt of some pungent scent. She had a blouse on under the fur coat. We found each other again on the bed, which consisted now only of a mattress.

The Gare de Lyon. Gay Orlov and Freddie were waiting at the entrance to the platform we were leaving from. Their numerous suitcases were piled on a trolley beside them. Gay Orlov had a wardrobe-trunk. Freddie was coming to terms with the porter and offered him a cigarette. Denise and Gay Orlov were talking and Denise asked her if the chalet Freddie had rented would be large enough for us all. The station was dark, except for the platform where we were standing, which was bathed in yellow light. Wildmer joined us, in a camel-hair coat which, as usual, flapped about his calfs. A felt hat was pulled down over his forehead. We had the luggage placed in our respective sleepers. We waited outside the carriage for our departure to be announced. Gay Orlov had recognized an acquaintance among the travellers taking this train but Freddie had asked her not to speak to anyone and draw attention to us.

I stayed a little while with Denise and Gay Orlov, in their compartment. The blinds were half pulled down and if I leaned forward I could look out and see that we were passing through the suburbs. It continued to snow. I embraced Denise and Gay Orlov and returned to my compartment, where Freddie had already settled in. Soon Wildmer paid us a visit. He had a compartment to himself for the time being, and he was hoping that no one would come until we had reached the end of our journey. He was afraid, in fact, of being recognized, as his picture had appeared a great deal in racing magazines some years back, at the time of his accident at the Auteuil races. We tried to reassure him, telling him that jockeys' faces were quickly forgotten.

Freddie and I stretched out on our bunks. The train had

picked up speed. We left our night-lights on and Freddie smoked nervously. He was a little anxious, because of the inevitable checks. I was, too, but I tried to hide it. Thanks to Rubirosa, the four of us, Freddie, Gay Orlov, Wildmer and I, had Dominican passports, but we could not be sure how effective they would be. Rubi himself had said so. We were at the mercy of some policeman or inspector more meddlesome than the others. Only Denise was safe. She was an authentic French citizen.

The train made its first stop. Dijon. The voice over the loudspeaker was muffled by the snow. We heard someone walking along the corridor. A compartment door was opened. Maybe someone was going into Wildmer's compartment. Then, the two of us were overcome by a fit of nervous laughter.

The train stopped for half an hour at Chalon-sur-Saône. Freddie had gone to sleep and I had turned out the night-light. I do not know why, but I felt more at ease in the dark.

I tried to think of something else, not to listen to the footsteps echoing in the corridor. People were speaking on the platform and I could make out some of the words of their conversation. They must have been standing in front of our window. One of them gave a phlegmy cough. Another whistled. The rhythmical noise of a passing train drowned their voices.

The door opened abruptly and the silhouette of a man in an overcoat was outlined against the light in the corridor. He swept the compartment from top to bottom with his pocket torch, to check how many of us there were. Freddie awoke with a start.

'Your papers . . . '

We handed him our Dominican passports. He examined them inattentively, then he gave them to someone next to him, whom we could not see because of the door. I closed my eyes. They exchanged several inaudible words.

He advanced one step into the compartment. He had our passports in his hand.

'You are diplomats?'

'Yes,' I replied mechanically.

After a moment or two, I remembered that Rubirosa had given us diplomatic passports.

Without a word, he handed us back our passports and closed the door.

We held our breath in the dark. We remained silent until the departure of the train. It got under way. I heard Freddie laugh. He switched on the light.

'Shall we go and see the others?' he said.

Denise and Gay Orlov's compartment had not been checked. We woke them up. They could not understand why we were so excited. Then Wildmer joined us, his face solemn. He was still trembling. He too had been asked if he were a 'Dominican diplomat' when he had shown his passport, and had not dared answer, for fear that among the plainclothes policemen and inspectors there might be some race-goer who would recognize him.

The train slipped through a white, snow-covered countryside. How gentle this landscape was, how friendly. Seeing these sleeping houses, I felt light-headed and confident for the first time.

It was still night when we arrived at Sallanches. A bus and a large black car were standing in front of the station. Freddie, Wildmer and I carried the suitcases, while two men took charge of Gay Orlov's wardrobe-trunk. There were about ten of us travellers who were taking the bus to Megève and the driver and two porters were piling the cases into the back when a fair-haired man, the same one Gay Orlov had noticed at the Gare de Lyon, the night before, approached her. They exchanged a few words in French. Later, she told us he was a distant relation, a Russian whose first name was

Kyril. He pointed to the large black car with someone waiting at the wheel, and offered to take us to Megève. But Freddie declined the offer, saying he preferred to take the bus.

It was snowing. The bus drove slowly and the black car passed us. The road we were on sloped and the chassis trembled at each gear change. I wondered if we would not break down before Megève. What did it matter? As the night gave way to a white, fleecy fog, through which the pine trees barely showed, I told myself that no one would come looking for us here. We were in no danger. We were gradually becoming invisible. Even our town clothes, which might have attracted attention – Wildmer's camel-hair coat and his navy-blue felt hat, Gay's leopard-skin, Freddie's russet coat, his green scarf and his large black and white golfing shoes – melted into this fog. Who knows? Perhaps we would end up evaporating altogether. Or we would merge with the mist which covered the windows, this stubborn mist which you could not wipe off. How could the driver get his bearings? Denise had fallen asleep and her head rested on my shoulder.

The bus stopped in the middle of the square, in front of the town hall. Freddie had our luggage lifted on to a sleigh that was waiting there and we went to get something warm to drink in a patisserie near the church. The place had just opened and the lady who served us seemed astonished to see such early customers. Or was it Gay Orlov's accent and our town clothes? Wildmer marvelled at everything. He did not yet know the mountains, nor was he familiar with winter sports. His forehead pressed against the window, his mouth hung open, he watched the snow falling on to the war memorial and the Megève town hall. He questioned the lady as to how the ski-lift worked and whether he could sign up for skiing lessons.

The chalet was called 'The Southern Cross'. It was a large, dark wood structure, with green shutters. I believe Freddie had rented it from one of his Parisian friends. It overlooked a bend in the road and could not be seen from there, as it was protected by a screen of pine trees. One reached it from the road, along a winding track. As for this road, it continued to climb, but I was never curious enough to find out just where. Denise's and my room was on the second floor and from the window, over the tops of the pines, we had a view of the whole village of Megève. When the weather was good, I practised spotting the church tower, the pale yellow patch made by a hotel at the foot of Rochebrune, the bus station and the skating rink, and, at the far end, the cemetery. Freddie and Gay Orlov occupied a room on the ground floor, next to the living room, and to get to Wildmer's room, one had to go down another floor, as it was a semi-basement and his window, a bull's eye, was on ground level. But Wildmer himself had chosen to move in there – his burrow, as he called it.

At first, we did not leave the chalet. We played cards endlessly in the living room. My memory of this room is fairly precise. A woollen carpet. A leather wall-sofa, above which was a shelf of books. A low table. Two windows giving on to a balcony. A woman who lived in the vicinity took care of the shopping in Megève. Denise read detective novels she had found on the bookshelf. I too. Freddie let his beard grow and Gay Orlov made borsch for us every day. Wildmer had asked for *Paris-Sport* to be brought regularly from the village and he read it, huddled deep inside his 'burrow'. One afternoon, while we were playing bridge, he appeared, an expression of disgust on his face, brandishing this magazine. A reporter, surveying the outstanding events of the last ten years in the world of racing, had recalled, among other things: 'The spectacular accident, at Auteuil, of the English jockey, André Wildmer.' Several photographs illustrated the article, among which was one of Wildmer, tiny, smaller than a postage stamp. And it was this which threw him into a panic. Someone at Sallanches station or in Megève, in the patisserie near the church, might have recognized him; the woman who brought our provisions and did some housework might have identified him as 'the English jockey, André Wildmer'. Had he not, a week before our departure, received an anonymous telephone call, at his home, in the Square des Aliscamps? A silky voice had said: 'Hullo. Still in Paris, Wildmer?' There had been a burst of laughter and they hung up.

It did no good our telling him over and over that he was in no danger, since he was a 'Dominican subject'. He was in a terrible state of nerves.

One night, at about three in the morning, Freddie banged violently on the door of Wildmer's 'burrow', shouting: 'We know you are there, André Wildmer . . . We know that you are the English jockey, André Wildmer. Come out at once . . . '

Wildmer had not appreciated this joke and would not speak to Freddie for two days. Then they made it up.

Apart from this insignificant incident, utter calm reigned in the chalet, the first few days.

But gradually Freddie and Gay Orlov began to find our daily routines tedious. Wildmer himself, in spite of his fear that he would be recognized as 'the English jockey', was becoming restless. He was a sportsman, not used to inaction.

Freddie and Gay Orlov met 'people' during their walks in Megève. A lot of 'people', it seemed, had taken refuge here like us. They got together, organized 'entertainments'. We heard of it through Freddie, Gay Orlov and Wildmer, who lost no time joining in this night life. I was distrustful. I preferred to remain in the chalet with Denise.

However, we did on occasions go down to the village. We would leave the chalet at around 10 a.m. and take a path lined with small chapels. Sometimes we went into one and Denise lit a candle. Some of them were closed. We walked slowly so as not to slip on the snow.

Lower down, a stone cross stood in the centre of a kind of circus from which a very steep path descended. Half the path had wooden steps built into it, but the snow had covered them. I walked in front of Denise, so that I could catch her if she slipped. At the bottom of the path was the village. We walked down the main street, to the square in front of the town-hall, and passed the Hôtel du Mont-Blanc. A little further, on the right, rose the greyish concrete building of the post-office. There, we sent some letters to Denise's friends: Léon, Hélène who had lent us her apartment in the Rue Cambacérès . . . I had written to Rubirosa to tell him we had arrived safely, thanks to his passports, and advised him to join us, as he had told me, the last time we had seen each other at the legation, that he intended to 'settle down to a quiet life'. I gave him our address.

The road sloped upwards toward Rochebrune. Groups of children, accompanied by gym instructresses in navy-blue winter sports outfits, were coming out of all the hotels along the road. They carried skis or ice-skates over their shoulders. The resort hotels had, in fact, been requisitioned for the poorest children of the large cities several months ago. Before turning back, we watched from afar people crowding round the ski-lift booking-office window.

Above 'The Southern Cross', if you followed the sloping path through the pine trees, you arrived at a very low, one-storey chalet. This was where the woman who did our shopping lived. Her husband owned a few cows. He was caretaker of 'The Southern Cross' when the owners were away and had fitted up a large room in his chalet with a rudimentary bar, seating, and a billiard-table. One afternoon, Denise and I went up there to fetch some milk. He was not very welcoming, but when Denise saw the billiard-table, she asked him if she could play. At first he seemed surprised, then he relaxed. He told her to come and play whenever she liked.

We often went there in the evenings, after Freddie, Gay Orlov and Wildmer had left us to plunge into Megève's night life. They suggested we join them at the 'Team', or in some chalet for an 'entertainment among friends', but we preferred to go up there. George – this was the man's first name – and his wife awaited us. I think they liked us. We played billiards with him and two or three of his friends. Denise was the best player. I can still see her standing there, slender, holding the cue, I can still see her gentle Asiatic face, her limpid eyes, her chestnut hair with copper reflections in it, which tumbled in coils to her hips . . .

We used to chat until very late with George and his wife. George told us there would certainly be ructions one of these days, and identity checks, since many of the people who were in Megève as holiday makers were on a continual spree and attracting attention. We were not like the others. He and his wife would take care of us, in case of difficulties.

Denise had disclosed to me that 'George' reminded her of her father. We often made a wood fire. The hours passed in warmth and closeness, and we felt at home.

Sometimes when the others had left, we stayed alone at 'The Southern Cross'. We had the chalet to ourselves. I would like to be able to relive certain clear nights when we gazed down at the village which stood out sharply against the snow, so that it looked like a miniature village, a toy village in a shop window at Christmas. Those nights, everything seemed simple and reassuring and we dreamt of the future. We would settle here, our children would go to the village school, summer would come with the tinkling bells of the herds being led to pasture. We would lead a happy life, with no surprises.

On other nights, the snow fell and I felt I was suffocating. We would never be able to get away, Denise and I. We were prisoners, at the end of this valley, and the snow would gradually bury us. There was nothing more disheartening than these mountains which blocked out the horizon. Panic took over. Then, I would open the french windows and we would go out on to the balcony. I breathed the cold air scented by pine trees. I was no longer afraid. On the contrary, I felt detached, serenely melancholic, faced with this landscape. And what about us in it? It seemed to me that the echo of our movements, of our lives, was smothered by this cotton wool which fell in light flakes around us, on the church tower, on the skating rink and the cemetery, on the darker line of the road threading the valley.

And then Gay Orlov and Freddie started inviting people to the chalet in the evenings. Wildmer was no longer afraid of being recognized and turned out to be the life and soul of the party. Ten, often more, would turn up unexpectedly at around midnight, and the party which had begun in another chalet took on a new lease of life. We avoided them, Denise and I, but Freddie asked us to stay so graciously, that sometimes we accepted.

I can still visualize several of those people, dimly as through a mist. A lively, dark-haired man who was always inviting you to join him in a game of poker and who drove around in a car registered in Luxemburg; a certain 'André-Karl', blond, with a red sweater, his face tanned by long-distance skiing; another fellow, very hefty, decked out in black velvet, and in my memory endlessly circling, like a large bumble-bee . . . And a number of women – someone called 'Jacqueline', a 'Mrs Campan' – good looking, open-air types.

Sometimes, once things were under way, the light in

the living room would be switched off suddenly, or a couple would disappear into a bedroom.

And now, this 'Kyril', whom Gay Orlov had met at Sallanches station and who had offered us a ride in his car. A Russian, married to a very pretty Frenchwoman. I believe he traded in tins of paint and in aluminium. He often telephoned Paris from the chalet and I kept telling Freddie that these phone calls would attract attention, but Freddie, like Wildmer, had lost all sense of caution.

It was 'Kyril' and his wife who brought Bob Besson and a certain 'Oleg de Wrédé' to the chalet one evening. Besson was a ski instructor, some of whose clients had been celebrities. He practised ski jumping and his face was scarred by some bad falls he had had. He limped slightly. A small, dark man, a native of Megève. He drank, which did not prevent him from skiing from eight in the morning. Besides his work as an instructor, he occupied a position in the Service Corps, and in this capacity had the use of a car, the black saloon which I had noticed on our arrival in Sallanches. Wrédé, a young Russian whom Gay Orlov had met before in Paris, paid frequent visits to Megève. He seemed to be living on his wits, buying and selling tyres and spare parts, since he too phoned Paris from the chalet, and I kept hearing him calling a mysterious 'Comet Garage'.

Why did I strike up conversation with Wrédé that evening? Perhaps because he was so easily approachable. He had a candid look and there was something in-genuously high-spirited about him. He laughed at the drop of a hat. Attentive to the point of continually asking you if you 'were all right', if you 'would not like something to drink', if you 'would not rather sit on the settee than in this chair', if you had 'slept well last night?' . . . A way of drinking in your words, eyes wide open, brow wrinkled, as though you were the oracle pronouncing.

He had understood our position and was very soon asking me if we wanted to remain here, 'in the mountains', for long. When I answered that we had no choice in the matter, he announced in a low voice that he knew a way of slipping across the Swiss frontier. Would it interest me?

I hesitated a moment and said, it would.

He told me that one should reckon on 50,000 francs per person and that Besson was in on it. Besson and he would conduct us to a point near the frontier, where a friend of theirs, an experienced guide, would take over. They had got around ten people, whose names he mentioned, into Switzerland this way. There was time to think it over. He was returning to Paris but would be back the following week. He gave me a phone number in Paris: AUTeuil 54-73, where I could contact him if I came to a swift decision.

I spoke to Gay Orlov, Freddie and Wildmer about it. Gay Orlov seemed amazed that 'Wrédé' was involved in frontier crossings, since the impression she had had was of a light-hearted young man, who eked out a living buying and selling things. Freddie thought there was no point in leaving France, since our Dominican passports protected us. Wildmer, for his part, thought Wrédé had the look of a 'gigolo', though it was Besson he particularly disliked. He claimed that the scars on Besson's face were phoney and that he applied them himself each morning with make-up. Rivalry between sportsmen? No, he really could not stand Besson whom he called: 'Papier Mâché'. Denise, on the other hand, found Wrédé 'attractive'.

As it happens, we made up our minds very quickly. It was because of the snow. It did not stop snowing for a week. I again had that feeling of suffocation which I had had in Paris. I told myself that if I stayed here any longer, we would be trapped. I explained to Denise how I felt.

Wrédé returned the following week. We came to an arrangement and discussed the frontier crossing with him and Besson. Never had Wrédé seemed so warm, so trustworthy. His friendly way of tapping you on the shoulder, his pale eyes, his white teeth, his eagerness, all this pleased me, although Gay Orlov had often told me laughingly that you had to be careful with Russians and Poles.

Very early that morning, Denise and I fastened the straps of our cases. The others were still asleep and we did not want to waken them. I left a note for Freddie.

They were waiting for us by the kerb, in Besson's black car, the one I had seen in Sallanches. Wrédé was at the wheel, Besson next to him. I opened the boot myself to put in the luggage and Denise and I got into the back of the car.

Throughout the journey no one talked. Wrédé seemed nervous.

It was snowing. Wrédé drove slowly. We drove over narrow, mountain roads. The journey took a good two hours.

It was when Wrédé stopped the car and asked me for the money that I had a vague presentiment. I handed him the wads of notes. He counted them. Then he turned round to us and smiled. He said that now, as a precautionary measure, we would split up, to cross the frontier. I would go with Besson, he and Denise with the luggage. We would meet again, in an hour, at his friends', on the other side. He kept smiling. A strange smile that I still see in my dreams.

I got out of the car with Besson. Denise sat down in the front, next to Wrédé. I looked at her, and again I had that presentiment. I wanted to open the door and tell her to get out. The two of us would have gone off together. But I told myself I had an ultra-suspicious nature and was imagining things. Denise seemed confident and in good spirits. She blew me a kiss.

She was dressed, that morning, in a skunk-fur coat, a Jacquard pullover, and ski trousers that Freddie had lent her. She was twenty-six, chestnut-brown hair, green eyes, and 5 foot 4 inches tall. We did not have much luggage: two leather bags and a small dark-brown suitcase.

Wrédé, still smiling, started the engine. I waved to Denise who was leaning her head out of the lowered window. I watched the car as it pulled away. Soon, she was nothing but a very small, dark spot.

I started walking, following Besson. I looked at his back and the marks of his footsteps in the snow. Suddenly, he told me he was going to scout ahead, as we were approaching the frontier. He told me to wait for him.

After about ten minutes, I realized he was not coming back. Why had I led Denise into this trap? I did my utmost to brush aside the thought that Wrédé would abandon her too and that nothing would be left of either of us.

It kept snowing. I walked on, looking in vain for some landmark. I walked for hours and hours. And finally I lay down in the snow. All around me there was nothing but whiteness.

38

I got off the train at Sallanches. The sun was shining. A motor coach, its engine running, was waiting on the station square. One solitary taxi, a DS 19, was parked by the side of the road. I climbed into it.

'Megève,' I said to the driver.

He started the car. A man of about sixty, with iron-grey hair, who wore a threadbare lumber-jacket with a fur collar. He was sucking a sweet or pastille.

'Nice weather, isn't it?' he said.

'It is . . . '

I gazed out of the window and tried to recognize the road we were on, but without snow, it looked quite different. The sun on the pines and the meadows, the arching trees overhead, all these different greens surprised me.

'I don't recognize the road,' I said to the driver.

'You've been here before?'

'Yes, a long time ago . . . there was snow on the ground . . . '

'It's not the same with snow.'

He took a small, circular, metal box from his pocket and held it out to me.

'Would you like a Valda?'

'Thanks.'

He took one himself too.

'I stopped smoking a week ago . . . My doctor told me to suck Valdas . . . Do you smoke?'

'I've stopped too . . . Tell me . . . Are you from Megève?'

'Yes, sir.'

'I knew some people in Megève . . . I'd very much like to find out what happened to them . . . There was this fellow, Bob Besson, for example.'

He slowed down and turned to me.

'Robert? The instructor?'

'Yes.'

He shook his head.

'I went to school with him.'

'What happened to him?'

'He's dead. He was killed ski jumping, a few years ago.'

'Oh, I see . . . '

'He might have made something of himself . . . But . . . Did you know him?'

'Not too well.'

'Robert got spoilt early on, because of his clientele . . . '

He opened the metal box and swallowed a pastille.

'He was killed outright . . . jumping . . . '

The motor coach was following us, about 20 yards behind. A light-blue coach.

'He was very friendly with a Russian fellow, wasn't he?' I asked.

'A Russian? Besson, friendly with a Russian?'

He didn't see what I was getting at.

'You know, Besson wasn't really up to much . . . He'd the wrong attitude . . . '

I realized he was not going to say anything more about Besson.

'Do you know a chalet in Megève called "The Southern Cross"?'

'"The Southern Cross"? . . . There are lots of chalets called that . . . '

Again he offered me the box of pastilles. I took one.

'The chalet jutted out over a road,' I said.

'What road?'

Yes, what road? The road I remembered looked like any other mountain road. How could I find it again? And perhaps the chalet was no longer there. And even if it were . . .

I leant towards the driver. My chin brushed against the fur collar of his lumber-jacket.

'Take me back to Sallanches station,' I said.

He turned round. He seemed surprised.

'As you wish, sir.'

39

Subject: HOWARD DE LUZ. Alfred Jean.

Born at: Port-Louis (Mauritius), 30th July, 1912, to HOWARD DE LUZ, Joseph Simety and Louise, née FOUQUEREAUX.

Nationality: British (and American).

Mr Howard de Luz resided successively at:

The Château Saint-Lazare, Valbreuse (Orne)
23, Rue Raynouard, Paris 16
Hôtel Chateaubriand, 18, Rue du Circque, Paris 8
53, Avenue Montaigne, Paris 8
25, Avenue du Maréchal-Lyautey, Paris 16

Mr Howard de Luz, Alfred Jean, had no obvious profession, in Paris.

From 1934 to 1939, he evidently devoted himself to searching for and selling old furniture, on behalf of a Greek residing in France, called Jimmy Stern, and at this time paid a long visit to the United States, from where his grandmother originated.

It seems that Mr Howard de Luz, although a member of a French family from Mauritius, made use of dual nationality, British and American.

In 1950, Mr Howard de Luz left France to settle in Polynesia, on the Island of Padipi, near Bora Bora (Society Isles).

The following note was attached to this memorandum:

'Dear Sir, please forgive this delay in conveying the information we have managed to obtain on Mr Howard de Luz. It was very hard to find. Being a British (or American) national, Mr Howard de Luz left hardly any traces behind in our departments and agencies.

'With kind regards to you and to Hutte.

J.-P. Bernardy.'

40

'My dear Hutte, I will be leaving Paris next week for a Pacific island where I may possibly find a man who can give me some information about my former life. He is a childhood friend.

Until now everything has seemed so chaotic, so fragmented . . . Scraps, shreds have come to light as a result of my searches . . . But then that is perhaps what a life amounts to . . .

Is it really my life I'm tracking down? Or someone else's into which I have somehow infiltrated myself?

I'll write to you from there.

I hope all is well with you in Nice and that you have got the position in the library which you wanted so much, in that place which reminds you of your childhood.'

41

AUTeuil 54-73: COMET GARAGE – 5, Rue Foucault. Paris 16.

42

A street giving on to the quay, in front of the Trocadero gardens. It seems to me that Waldo Blunt, the American

pianist I had accompanied home and who was Gay
Orlov's first husband, lived in this street.

The garage had closed down a long time before, to
judge by the big, rusty, iron gate. Above the latter, on
the grey wall, you could still make out: COMET GARAGE,
even though the blue lettering was half obliterated.

On the first floor, to the right, a window with a
dangling, orange blind. A bedroom window? an office?
Had the Russian been in this room when I phoned
AUTeuil 54-73 from Megève? What was he doing at the
Comet Garage? How could I find out? It all seemed so
distant, as I stood in front of this deserted building . . .

I turned around and stood a moment on the quay. I
watched the cars passing and the lights, on the other
side of the Seine, near the Champ-de-Mars. Maybe some
part of my life still survived there, in a small apartment
overlooking the gardens, some person who had known
me and who still remembered me.

43

A woman is standing at one of the windows of a ground
floor apartment, on the corner of the Rue Rude and the
Rue de Saigon. The sun is shining and children are
playing ball outside on the pavement, a little way off.
The children keep shouting 'Pedro', because one of
them is called that and the others are challenging him
while continuing to play. And this 'Pedro', pronounced
in clear, ringing tones, echoes oddly in the street.

From her window, she cannot see the children.
Pedro. She knew someone called that, a long time ago.
She tries to remember when it was, while the cries, the
laughter and the dull thud of the ball rebounding

against a wall reach her. Ah, yes. It was when she was a fashion model, at Alex Maguy's. She had met a certain Denise, a blonde, rather Asiatic looking, who also worked in fashion. They took to each other straight away.

Denise lived with a man called Pedro. A South American, no doubt. She remembered that this Pedro, in fact, worked at a legation. A tall, dark man, whose features she remembered quite distinctly. She would still recognize him today, except he must have gained a few grey hairs since.

One evening, the two of them came to her place, in the Rue de Saigon. She had invited a few friends over to dinner. The Japanese actor and his wife with coral-blonde hair who lived nearby, in the Rue Chalgrin, Evelyne, a dark-haired woman she had known at Alex Maguy's, escorted by a pale young man, someone else – but she had forgotten who – and Jean-Claude, the Belgian who was courting her . . . The dinner had been a jolly affair. She had thought, what a handsome couple Denise and Pedro made.

One of the children catches the ball, hugs it to him and lopes off with large strides. She sees them passing her window on the run. Panting, the one holding the ball comes out into the Avenue de la Grande-Armée. He crosses the road, still hugging the ball. The others do not dare follow him and stand there, watching him running along the opposite pavement. He kicks the ball ahead of him. The sun is shining on the chrome of bicycles in the windows of the bicycle shops along the avenue.

He has forgotten the others. He runs on his own with the ball, and dribbles it, turning right into the Rue Anatole-de-la-Forge.

44

I pressed my brow to the port-hole. Two men were keeping watch on the bridge, chatting, and the moon-light gave their skins an ashen appearance. Finally they leant over the rails.

I could not sleep, even though there was no more swell. I kept looking through the photographs of us all, Denise, Freddie, Gay Orlov, and gradually they lost their reality, as the boat continued on its way. Had they ever existed? I remembered what I had been told about Freddie's activities in America. He had been the 'confidant of John Gilbert'. And I could see them: two men walking side by side in the neglected grounds of a villa, past a tennis court covered with dead leaves and broken twigs, the taller of the two men – Freddie – leaning towards the other who must have been speaking in a low voice and was undoubtedly John Gilbert.

Later I heard a scuffle, bursts of laughter and voices in the ship's gangways. They were arguing over a trumpet, who was to play the opening bars of 'Auprès de ma blonde'. The door of the cabin next to mine slammed. There were several people in it. Again there were bursts of laughter, the clinking of glasses, fast breathing, a soft, drawn out moan . . .

Someone was prowling the corridors, ringing a little bell and repeating in the high-pitched voice of a choir-boy that we had crossed the Line.

45

Over there was a succession of red navigation lights, which seemed at first to be suspended in air, before one realized that they followed the line of a bank. The dark-blue, silken shape of a mountain. Calm waters, after passing the reefs.

We were entering in the roads of Papeete.

46

I had been recommended to see a certain Fribourg. He had been living in Bora Bora for thirty years and made documentary films about the Pacific islands which he usually showed in Paris, at the Salle Pleyel. He was extremely knowledgeable about the South Sea Islands.

I did not even have to show him the photograph of Freddie. He had met him on several occasions when he berthed at the Island of Padipi. He described him to me as a man of over six feet, who never left his island, or if he did, went out alone on his boat, a schooner, on which he made long trips through the Tuamotu Archipelago, and even as far as the Marquesas.

Fribourg offered to take me to the Island of Padipi. We embarked on a sort of fishing vessel. We were accompanied by a fat Maori who never moved more than an inch from Fribourg's side. I believe they lived together. A strange couple, this little man with the manners of a former chief scout, in worn, golf plus fours and a sport's shirt, and wearing glasses with metal frames, and the big bronzed Maori. The latter was dressed in a grass skirt and a bodice of pale blue cotton fabric. During the crossing, he told me in a soft voice that as a youth he had played football with Alain Gerbault.

47

On the island, we followed a turf-covered path, lined with coconut palms and breadfruit trees. Here and there, a white, breast-high wall marked the boundaries of a garden, in the middle of which stood a house – always the same style – with a veranda and corrugated iron roof, painted green.

We came out into a wide meadow surrounded by barbed wire. Along the left-hand side ran a line of hangars, among which was a three-storey building of a rosy beige colour. Fribourg explained that it was an old aerodrome, constructed by the Americans during the Pacific war, and that this was where Freddie lived.

We entered the three-storey building. On the ground floor, a room with a bed and a mosquito-net, a desk and a wicker armchair. A door led into a rudimentary bathroom.

On the first and second floors, the rooms were empty and there were panes missing in the windows. Some piles of rubbish in the corridors. A military map of the South Pacific had been left hanging on one of the walls.

We returned to the room which must have been Freddie's. Brown-feathered birds slipped through the half open window and perched, in tight ranks, on the bed, the desk and bookshelf near the door. More and more came. Fribourg told me these were Moluccan blackbirds and that they gnawed through everything, paper, wood, even the walls of houses.

A man entered the room. He was wearing a grass skirt and had a white beard. He spoke to the fat Maori who was sticking to Fribourg like a shadow and the fat man translated, swaying slightly from side to side. About two weeks ago, the schooner on which Freddie had set off for the Marquesas had fetched up on the island's coral reefs, and Freddie was no longer on board.

He asked us if we wished to see the boat and led us to the edge of the lagoon. The boat was there, its mast broken, while, to protect it, old lorry tyres had been hung on its side.

Fribourg announced that once we got back, we would ask for searches to be made. The fat Maori in the pale blue bodice was talking to the other one in a very shrill voice. They seemed to be uttering little cries. Soon I stopped paying any attention to them.

I do not know how long I remained by the edge of the lagoon. I thought about Freddie. No, he simply could not have vanished at sea. No doubt, he had decided to cut his last ties and must be hiding out on an atoll. I would find him in the end. And besides, there was one last thing I would have to try: to return to my old address in Rome, Via delle Botteghe Oscure, 2.

Evening had come. The lagoon was fading gradually, as its greenness was reabsorbed. Greyish mauve shadows still moved on the water, in a dim phosphorescence.

Mechanically, I had taken out of my pocket the photographs of us all which I had wanted to show Freddie, and among them the photo of Gay Orlov as a little girl. I had not noticed until then that she was crying. One could tell by the wrinkling of her brows. For a moment, my thoughts transported me far from this lagoon, to the other end of the world, to a seaside resort in Southern Russia where the photo had been taken, long ago. A little girl is returning from the beach, at dusk, with her mother. She is crying for no reason at all, because she would have liked to continue playing. She moves off into the distance. She has already turned the corner of the street, and do not our lives dissolve into the evening as quickly as this grief of childhood?